Pride Publishing books by Megan Slayer:

I0570379

Constant
Permanent
Vaulting
Drive my Car

What's his Passion?
Wild Card

Anthologies
Out of Bounds: Crossing the Line
Aim High: Lifetime Hitch

What's his Passion?

WILD CARD

MEGAN SLAYER

Wild Card
ISBN # 978-1-78651-945-0
Copyright Megan Slayer 2016
Cover Art by Posh Gosh ©Copyright April 2016
Interior text design by Claire Siemaszkiewicz
Pride Publishing

Published in 2016 by Pride Publishing, Newland House, The Point, Weaver Road, Lincoln, LN6 3QN, United Kingdom.

Pride Publishing is a subsidiary of Totally Entwined Group Limited.

WILD CARD

Dedication

For CD who told me not to give up.
For SM because you're awesome.
For JPZ—you're my wild card.

Chapter One

Just a few more movies and he'd be done. Kris Hunter curled the pages of the script in both hands. A dull ache started behind his eyes. He'd become popular in the adult film industry but desperately wanted to get out. Starring in porn paid the bills, but didn't soothe his primal need to create. Shouting 'take that cock up your ass now' got old after a while.

He raked his fingers through his hair and read through his lines again. There wasn't much to the script. A few lines about getting to know his playmate, then naked time. God. He'd been asked to star in another first experience flick. He should've known better.

If he wanted to get out of the business, he'd have to star in a few more films and bank up the rest of the money he needed. Time to get his head into the game.

"It's your first time? A sexy man like you? Can't be."

Kris nodded. He needed to get into the headspace of a guy who wanted to hook up with a younger man. Gag. At twenty-seven, he wasn't that fucking old. Still, he needed the money to fund his dream. He formed an image of his costar in his mind. Although he wasn't attracted to the other performer, Kris did his best to act the part.

"That's right," Kris murmured. "You know how to kiss."

His costar, Garig Ross, strode into the living room. "Are you actually practicing your lines?"

Kris opened his eyes. He hadn't realized he'd closed them. "Go fuck yourself."

"Now that's not the way to entice me to want to be fucked by you." Garig shrugged out of his street clothes. Unlike Kris, Garig seemed to love being nude. He folded his jeans and tucked his things into his duffle bag. "You're supposed to make me at least kind of want to be with you."

"I don't want to be *here* or with *you*." Kris dropped the script onto his bag. "I'm tired of these movies."

"So?" Garig shook out the ripped denim. He waved the jeans around. "This won't cover my ass."

"That's the point. You're supposed to look young, interested, and green as hell but ready to take a seven-inch cock up your tight ass." Kris rolled his eyes. "You're young, but you are no virgin."

"Don't you know it." Garig stepped into the jeans, then slid his cowboy boots back on. He admired his ass in the mirror. "Papa likes what he sees."

If Kris had been on the prowl for a date and wasn't picky, he might have hooked up with Garig for real. The guy was handsome. From his perfectly styled hair combed to appear as if he'd rolled straight out of bed, down his chiseled body to his sculpted legs, he personified sexy. Most guys wanted to fuck him — except Kris.

He'd made fifteen flicks with Garig. None of them endeared Garig to him. The guy might be hot, but he was also a hot mess. He dropped his pants for everyone and God only knew if he was careful.

"We're going to do this thing." Garig wriggled into the vest. His pierced nipples glinted in the light. "What are you saving all that money for?"

"Nothing." Kris glanced in the mirror and slicked his hair back. He never wore his hair forward in the films. The combed-back style made him feel like the character rather than himself. Maybe that was crazy, but he preferred having the bit of separation.

He tucked his wallet, keys and phone into his bag, then stripped down to his running pants and the tank top. According to the script, he was supposed to start out on his balcony. Garig would be on the balcony next door, flirting.

He closed his eyes again. Three more films and he'd have enough money. A momentary vision popped into his brain. He didn't want to be in front of the camera without his clothes. He'd be making actual movies with plots and good actors. Even if he had to fund the damn thing himself, he was going to be a real actor in a real movie. He opened his eyes. *Get the film done and move forward.*

"All right. Let's go," the director said. He pointed to Kris. "Your condoms and lube are beside the bed."

"You'd make so much more money if you'd just do these bare." Garig shrugged. "I'm raking it in."

"I'm fine with what I'm doing." At least when they worked, he knew he was safe. Kris made his way through the bedroom and stopped on the balcony.

"You're going to chat him up. Stick to the script if you want, but you have to say he's a hot piece of ass and you want to do him," the director said. He clapped Kris on the shoulder. "Just make it sound intelligent and like you really want him."

God. Kris stood on the balcony and gripped the railing. Three years before, he'd have considered throwing himself over the edge. Too many demons remained with him. He shook off the black feelings and focused on the job at hand.

"Ready? Action." The director pointed to him. The camera clicked.

Time to shine. Kris gripped the railing again and stared at the city below. The palm trees waved in the slight breeze. Cars zipped down the street.

"There is nothing happening in this city." He sighed. "Nothing."

Garig appeared on his own balcony. "I don't know about that."

"Oh?" Kris leaned against his railing. "You're new."

"I am, and in more ways than you know." Garig grinned. "Where's your boyfriend?"

Ah. They weren't following the script at all. Kris folded his hands. "I'm single. You?"

"Ready to mingle," Garig replied. "Let me come over."

"The door is open." Kris nodded toward the other side of the apartment. "Let yourself in."

"Cut," the director shouted. "Reset. Good take."

Kris groaned. He knew what to do next. Hell, he'd been a professional in the adult world since he'd turned twenty-one, six years ago. But he wanted more out of life. Unfortunately, life didn't want him to graduate beyond the blow jobs and anal sex on camera. He thought back to his high school career. He'd nailed the Shakespeare plays and the dippy romantic comedies the drama club insisted on presenting every spring. He loved the rush of performing and the grit of having to work with others for that play to turn out right.

He glanced over at Garig. The only acting he'd get to do now would be to appear to be interested in what was going on. Another player strolled into the room. Not a grip or a camera man. Kris studied the new guy. Young and very eager. The kid practically bounced over to the director.

"Who?" Kris heard the director ask. "Oh. Over there. You know what to do."

The kid crossed the room and stood in front of Kris. He didn't say anything, just stared at him.

"Hello." Kris backed away from the guy. "What do you want?"

"I'm your fluffer." The guy batted his eyelashes. His brown eyes twinkled. "I'm supposed to get you ready."

"Yeah." Kris backed up another foot. "No. I'm fine. I'll manage."

"How else am I supposed to learn about this business if I don't work my way up?"

"Who are you again?" Kris asked.

"Fain." The guy crinkled his nose. "Rhymes with vain. I'm not, but you know. It's catchy." He chewed on his bottom lip, accentuating the piercing and small patch of hair growing below his lip. "I'm old enough to be here. I'm twenty-two."

"Well, Fain, thanks but no thanks. I don't need…fluffing." Kris sidestepped Fain and stood beside the bed. He prided himself on not needing help in the bedroom. He might not be interested in the partner he was about to fuck, but he had a good enough bank of mental images to pull from to get him through.

"Fain, I need you back here." The director yanked Fain out of the way. "Garig, you stroll in from this door and Kris, I want you waiting on the bed. Go for the come hither look. You're ready, you're willing, but he's got to come to you."

"That's my motivation?" Kris asked and snorted. He bit back another sigh. Damn, this was getting old. He stretched out on the mattress and crossed his ankles. He propped himself up on one elbow. "I'm ready."

"Garig?" The director jumped behind the camera and snapped the clapper bar. "Where are you?"

"Ready." Garig grinned from the doorway. "Whenever you are."

Kris freed his mind of his problems and focused on the film. *Get it done and get out of there.* He smiled at Garig. "I see you've found your way in."

"What's a guy like you see in a guy like me?" Garig asked. He shrugged out of the vest. "Tell me."

"A horny bastard." Kris grabbed Garig's hand. He blocked out the actual act of licking Garig's dick and hole. He feigned interest in Garig's job of sucking him to erect. Maybe he was screwing himself over, but he could've called the scene in. He donned the rubber, then dribbled lube over Garig's ass. In seconds he was inside and thrusting.

Kris didn't actually count the minutes, but he'd be willing to guess the director wasn't getting enough shots by the amount of cursing going on in the background.

"God damn it. You know there's going to be music, but I swear you're pissing me off intentionally, Kris." The director snapped the clapper board. "Cut." He directed his frustration at Kris. "I need better close-ups. You look more like you're going to be sick than that you're enjoying this."

"Maybe I'm not." Kris rested his hands on his hips. "Sorry."

"No, you're not," the director replied, his tone flat.

"I'm not, but hold up. Isn't this flick actually supposed to be about Garig and his...journey? The viewer wants to see things from his perspective and be in his position. I'll get more into this, but you should focus on him more." Kris nodded, as if the gesture would convince the director to go along with his line of thinking.

"You're a dick." The director wiped the sweat off his brow. "Fine. But act more like you're getting off on what he's doing."

"I will," Kris said, not really meaning his words. He'd done a piss-poor job of portraying his interest. Damn. He'd have to really focus if he wanted to come across as at least a little excited. He stroked his dick, then swatted Garig's ass. Soon, he'd be done taking his clothes off for money. Soon.

Half an hour later, the director yelled cut for the last time. "I've got what I need to get this film done. Next time, Garig, don't act quite so cartoony and Kris—try to want to be here. That's a wrap."

Kris darted into the bathroom to ditch the rubber and clean up. He tossed the used condom into the waste bin, then wetted a washcloth with warm water. He stared at himself in the mirror as the water heated up. The lines around his eyes had deepened a bit more and he noticed two strands of gray hair at his temples. Fuck. He wasn't allowed to look old yet.

"So." Garig stood behind him and made faces in the mirror. "You're never going to bottom? Ever?"

"Nope." He cleaned off his dick, happy to get the grime of the shoot off his body. Still, the quick wipe-down wasn't enough. He switched on the water in the shower. He'd have to hurry if he wanted to make his next appointment, but he'd manage.

"Why?" Garig sobered. "Seriously. The viewers want to see you bottom." He tapped the glass shower panel. "They want you to beg someone else to fuck you."

"I don't want to and I don't have to, so I'm not going to." Besides, he needed to control the action. When he allowed himself to let go, bad things happened. He lathered his body, then rinsed. Thank God, he'd been given a decent head of hair. Wash and go actually fit his style and worked for him.

"You'd make so much more money if you'd at least go bare. I'm clean. You can fuck me all you want, but bareback. Hell, you're the cleanest-cut guy in the herd. I'd let you fuck me any day."

"I'd rather not. I'm doing well with the plan I've got going," Kris said and turned off the water. He grabbed the nearest towel. "I'm happy and that's what matters."

Garig stepped into a pair of boxer shorts. "You're lying."

Kris left the bathroom and headed back to the living room for his bag. "I'm not." Not completely. He'd faked his way through the shoot and pretended to be interested when he'd been given the assignment to do the film. Maybe he was lying — to himself.

"Dude, this job is about pleasing the fans and making money. You're being ignorant. You could not only win awards for your performances, but rake in the dough." Garig plopped onto the couch. "Serious. You need to take the next step."

"No." He slid his boxers and jeans on, then wrestled into his socks.

"Why? Are you still actually thinking about going straight? You know studios won't hire ex-porn stars. We're not bankable and too risky. The public wants us to be having sex, not trying to date the girl-next-door." Garig crossed his legs and propped his feet on the coffee table. "Truth."

"I'm an actor, not a porn star." Kris yanked his shirt down over his head and stuck his arms through the sleeves. He finger-combed his hair. "I'm getting out of here."

"Out of the business or the house? The house, I'm sure. The business?" Garig asked. "Not gonna happen. You're *so* not an actor."

Kris rolled his eyes and picked up his bag. He'd left his cowboy boots in the bedroom. Once he retrieved the footwear, he left the apartment. He shivered. After each shoot, he needed a shower to wash off the ick.

"One day," he chanted. "One day." He hurried down to his car, then slid behind the wheel. If he made all the green lights and didn't get stuck in traffic, he'd make it to the casting call on time.

Half an hour later, he pulled into a parking spot in front of the Liberty Studios building. He'd been to the building half a dozen times for various other roles. Of the fifty parts he'd gone out for, he'd landed one. The role of pilot number three in a war flick. Unfortunately for him, he'd ended up on the cutting room floor. Not a great way to start a career in serious film.

He dug through his bag for the script. The call today was for a guy in his late twenties with a dark past. He had to portray grief and sadness while staying cool and collected. His backstory included being assaulted and hardened by life. Kris glanced at his reflection in the rearview mirror. If he combed his hair forward and knotted his eyebrows, he could pull off intensity. He knew how it felt to grow up angry. He *owned* that role.

"You can do this," he muttered to himself. "You can absolutely do this." Kris climbed out of his car and locked the vehicle, then headed into the building. He signed in. The receptionist told him where to wait. His hands shook and he wished he'd brought mints. Twenty other guys just like him waited too. He held the script in his hands, crinkling the paper.

He'd never know if he could move beyond porn if he didn't put himself out there. Who knew? He might actually land the role, or even a guy who liked him for more than his body. Wishing for all that was a little much, but fuck it. Time to find out if he was ready to leave his past behind him and move forward with his life.

* * * *

Zayn slapped his notebook shut. Christ. He'd seen nearly fifty actors already and didn't believe he'd spotted one that would even remotely fit the role. He gathered the stack of dossiers on the rest of the actors coming in. He'd spent the last fifteen years in the movie business, seven of which he'd worked as a casting director. He knew who he wanted for the roles he cast. He had a sixth sense about the actors. Who could handle something deeper and who just wanted a paycheck.

After looking at so many actors, he didn't want to search any longer. No one was right for the depth of the character.

"What's wrong with that batch?" Myron, the producer, asked. "Good God. We've seen a thousand people."

"Not a thousand." Zayn folded his arms. "None of them are right. These guys are better for romantic comedies and bro pictures. This role will take more guts than anything."

"You don't want to do your job." Myron snorted. "I don't trust you."

"I'm damn good at my job," Zayn said. He focused on the papers, not the producer. He knew what he was doing and his choices were always spot-on.

"You bring in people I didn't think could do the role." The veins stuck out in Myron's forehead.

"Who usually turn out to be perfect," Zayn snapped. "My track record speaks for itself." He'd cast actors in movies that had garnered multiple awards.

"Whatever." Myron shoved his chair into the table. "I'm going out for a smoke."

"Have fun," Zayn called. He and Myron had never been good friends and when they had to work together, the claws certainly came out. Myron had one idea for the movie and Zayn always had another. The fact that Zayn's wild cards worked out most often seemed to stick in Myron's craw.

"So what are we going to do?" Jordan asked. He'd signed on to direct the picture and shared the same vision for the secondary character as Zayn.

"We bring in the others." Zayn slid the pages apart. "A couple of them appear promising."

"They're all that bad?"

"No, but none of them have shown the spark you want. Am I right?" Zayn asked.

"I agree." Jordan stood and stretched. "I need a break. You okay with going through a few on your own? I trust your judgment. If Myron doesn't, then fuck him. He's never happy." He winked, then strolled out of the room, leaving Zayn alone.

Why in the hell did they bring me in if only Jordan agrees with me? Zayn rubbed his temples. The others didn't understand the importance of the role of Rock Magnus. The guy was fucked up. He'd been assaulted as a kid to the point of making him permanently angry. He didn't settle down with one woman in favor of having as many as possible and without discussion. Someone who tried to portray the character with too much comedy would ruin the role.

He tapped the pages together. The next guy—on paper—seemed closer to right than the others. Now if he would just show up.

As if on cue, an actor strode into the room. The guy stood erect and looked Zayn in the eye. Heat stirred in Zayn's belly. Damn. If he wasn't completely averse to dating actors, he'd snap this guy up in a heartbeat. The guy ambled like a soccer player, with his center of gravity in his hips, not his chest. He'd brushed his dark hair forward, giving him an air of mystery. His blue eyes sparkled. He appeared to need a shave, too.

Zayn bit back a groan. The guy physically fit the role of Rock, but could he pull off the acting to get the part right? He'd garnered Zayn's attention and not in a professional way. Why couldn't Zayn meet guys like him in the clubs? Maybe then he'd be able to ditch his self-imposed celibacy.

"Hi." The man stuck out his hand. "I'm Kris Hunter. I'm auditioning for the role of Rock Magnus. I've got the script with me."

"Good to meet you." Zayn shook hands with Kris. A firm handshake. *Nice.* "It would appear the panel is just me for right now. Why don't you go to the second scene and read against me?" *Or lean against me and stuff my ass with your dick...* Zayn snapped his lips shut. Please God, he hoped he hadn't said that last bit out loud. He needed to get laid and fast so he could focus on his job.

"Sure." Kris flipped through the thin script. He cleared his throat. "What do you mean, I can't have her? Bullshit. She's mine just as much as Helene's mine."

Damn. He had a smooth voice, almost velvety. Zayn suppressed a shiver. He smoothed the script open. *Focus.* "My girls aren't here for you to take."

"Because you know they want to go with me." Kris bobbed his eyebrows. "What can I say? I'm good with the ladies."

"You are," Zayn replied. "I'll have to keep my eye on you." The man was lethal. He drew the viewer in with his voice and his look. The more he spoke, the more Zayn knew he'd found his Rock.

"Eye? Shit." Kris shrugged. He patted his hip as if he were patting a firearm. "What are you going to do about McCloskey? I can't have him running loose."

"It's under control." Zayn closed the script. He propped his feet on the desk. "Good job. Why don't you sit? We'll do the open discussion part of the reading."

Kris dragged a chair up to the table and did as told. His hands trembled. Not much, but enough for Zayn to notice.

"Nervous?" Zayn asked. He liked to think he could read people well, but something about this guy made him pause.

"I am. I've never gotten this far in an audition for a larger film. I don't have tons of experience on the big screen. Two roles as an extra in a crowd scene and as Pilot number three in *Stampede*. Unfortunately, Myron Bixby went in another direction and I ended up on the cutting room floor. I'm either too tall for the role or not what the casting director is interested in...or something."

"Have you got your résumé?"

"I do." Kris produced a sheet of paper from his messenger bag. "This isn't my first call with you."

Zayn paused. He'd seen Kris? No. He scanned the résumé. Little by little, he recalled the information. Twenty-seven years old and in film for six of those years. He'd done plenty of commercials and a few crowd scenes. Why hadn't he made more of a splash?

"Three weeks ago I auditioned for you on the Chicago movie. Turned me down." Kris grinned. As brooding and dark as he'd appeared a few moments ago, when he smiled his boyish qualities shone through.

"Huh. I saw more than two hundred men for that role." Zayn dog-eared the paper. "Well, I'm impressed with this reading. I'm not guaranteeing a call back, but I will keep in touch. This information is all current, correct?"

"It is." Kris stood and offered his hand again. "Thank you."

"You're welcome." *Manners too. What a catch!* Zayn shook hands again. When Kris left the room, Zayn watched his ass wiggle. Just enough bounce to grab, but not too much. A low rumble built in his throat. Part of him wanted to see that ass naked. One day…probably on set. The rest of him chided himself for being so horny. God. He was there to cast a role, not pick up a date.

Jordan strolled into the room a few moments after Kris left. He pulled his chair out. "Did you see one while I was gone?"

"I did." Zayn slid Kris' résumé over to the director. "I know eyeballing him isn't enough, but I've got a gut feeling about him. He's got the velvety voice that's a cross between sexy and dangerous. You want to believe what he says, but you know there's a good chance he's going to pull a fast one on you. He read lines with me and it was good."

"Sounds like you're convinced." Jordan turned the page around. "We've got a problem."

"What?"

"He's in porn." He tapped the paper. "See? That's where he's getting most of his experience. Doesn't bother me that he's done skin flicks, but Myron will never go for it."

"That makes sense then. He said something about getting booted out of a Bixby picture. Think Myron found out and bounced him?" Zayn twiddled with the edge of the résumé page. "He's got the chops for the part."

"You're sure?" Jordan asked.

"I am. I want to bring him back to read in front of everyone." He debated his options. If he had Kris come back, he'd have to keep Kris' prior jobs quiet. He wanted Myron to consider the actor for his skills, not his other work — not in this situation.

"Well, I'll back you up. I know your choices. If you're sure, then I am too. We'll omit some details to Myron and see what happens." Jordan sighed. "But first, we've got to listen to the other thirty guys waiting in the other room."

"Fine." Zayn sat back in his chair and folded his arms. He'd made up his mind, but he knew damn well Myron would shoot down his choice. He listened through the next ten auditions. Two of the actors had the right visual appeal, but not the swagger. Another had the swagger to boot, but not the rest. Even with a wardrobe upgrade and a different haircut, the actor wouldn't be right.

Three actors showed up at the same time. Each were known for high-profile roles in other films. The actors read the selection he'd read with Kris. Maybe he was losing his mind or his touch, but he kept going back to the interaction with Kris. He wanted to hear that voice speaking to him at night. Wanted to feel those arms around him when he slept.

Holy fuck. He'd known the guy for less than five minutes and was already turned on. What the hell? This wasn't his style. He waited and moved methodically. Going gangbusters, especially with actors, always ended in disaster and yet, there he was, wondering what it would feel like to be with Kris.

The actors left with little fanfare. Myron walked them out of the room, then returned to the table. He turned his notepad around.

"We've seen about a hundred or so actors." Myron tapped the papers. "I've got a shortlist of three actors I want to bring back. What about you, Zayn? Did any of them stand out for you?"

He debated his answer. He knew what he wanted to say, but didn't want to chance losing the right guy for the role. "Tony Bosa is good. He's a second choice. I'd like to hear him read again, plus Bobby Little. He was good and had the right visual appeal. The one I'm dying to bring back is Kris Hunter. There's something about him. With everything he's got going for him...I think he's the right one, but I need a second read-through to be sure."

"Which one was he?" Myron flipped through the résumés. "Did I see him?"

"No. He came in while you were on your break." Zayn toyed with his watch. If he acted nonchalantly, then maybe Myron wouldn't see the excitement racing through his veins.

"Do I know of him?" Myron frowned. "I've heard that name before."

"You've worked with him before. He was part of *Stampede*. Sounds like you cut him before the end of editing." Zayn shifted in his seat. "He's got the chops."

"I agree. He nailed the part and looks it." Jordan folded his hands. "I wouldn't be so certain, but I saw him. He's good."

Zayn bit back a snort. If he didn't know Jordan better, he'd have thought Jordan really had been there to watch the audition.

"Fine. Put the list together and I'll have my secretary call each of the actors." Myron shook his head. "I hate these sessions." He stood and shoved his chair in to the desk. His grumbles could be heard down the hallway as he left.

"That went well," Jordan said and grunted. "He's an old bastard."

"Nah. He's good at what he does. He knows how to make the movies shine—with the right amount of money. Our problem is that the actor I want isn't going to fit Myron's mold. Unless he's willing to bow to Myron or to change his name…he won't have a chance." Zayn leaned forward and rested his elbows on his knees. "I know I want him."

"No shit." Jordan clapped Zayn on the shoulder. "I haven't seen you this hung up on someone in a long time. You need this, even if he's not the one we end up hiring. Think he'd go out with you?"

"Are you cracked? I don't date actors. He's hot, but he's not my type." Zayn shook his head. He knew better than to try to convince Jordan otherwise, but still. He wasn't going to date Kris.

"Keep telling yourself that bullshit. I know you want him. You need a good dick up your ass to get your mind off Kris' ass." Jordan grinned. "Come on. It's late and I'm hungry. Let's get some dinner. I don't really want to audition the actresses on an empty stomach. Too much drama."

Zayn snorted. "Why? Because you think they want to sleep with you?"

"Because I'll have to explain to my wife why I smell like fifteen kinds of perfume." Jordan laughed and slapped Zayn's back. "Come on. Food is calling my name."

Zayn left his seat and pushed the chair up to the table. He'd lost his mind. He did want Kris—more than he cared to admit out loud. He imagined a night with the hunky actor. The guy would definitely have skills. He did porn. While Zayn and the others sat at dinner, he turned the sound down on his phone and searched Kris' name on his Internet browser. A hundred links came back in the list and all included Kris' likeness. The man was prolific, just like his résumé claimed. Zayn glanced up at his supper companions. He wanted to watch at least one of the short films, but that would have to wait until later. First, he had to get through supper. But he knew exactly who he wanted to play the role of Rock—Kris.

Chapter Two

Kris parked his car in the driveway of his condo and switched off the engine. The ride home had taken longer than he wanted, but at least he was back at his own place with silence. He glanced over at the neighbor's front yard. The dog, a black pit bull no more than two years old, was chained to the tree...again. Kris sighed. The dog spent more time locked outside than he was allowed inside. If he wouldn't end up busted for theft, Kris would've rescued the dog. No food, only rainwater and no shelter other than the shade of the tree. Who did such cruel things?

He'd bought a small bag of dog food and took some to the dog when the owner wasn't home. Someone had to take care of the poor pooch. The way things appeared, he'd have to bring another bowl of food over to the dog, Nugent.

His phone rang, breaking his concentration. Kris answered, but continued to watch the dog. "Hello?"

"There's my golden boy — or should I say my raven-haired star. How're ya feeling tonight?"

Great. Kris bit back a groan. Donovan, yet another director. "Which skin flick do you want me for this time?" He hadn't worked with Donovan in six months and for good reason. Donovan got off on producing domination pictures. Kris knew his way around a bondage scene and had training as a Dominant, but those weren't his style of films. He didn't mind a little spanking, dirty talk and soft bondage. Hell, he loved those, but the rest wasn't for him.

"You said you wanted to act," Donovan said. "I've got a plum role for you, with acting and it's only going to take one day. There's an actual script and it's not something jotted on a napkin. I promise. Oh, and no BDSM. The storyline doesn't call for it and I can't work it in."

Thank God. "Okay, so it's softer on the porn scale. When is this filming going to take place?" He wasn't truly that interested, but if the shoot paid enough, he'd be even closer to his goal.

"Tomorrow."

"Are you for real? I can't do it tomorrow." Not all-day filming anyway. He stopped short of admitting what he was actually going to be doing. Donovan would have a fit. He hated for his performers to leave the business and let them know in no uncertain terms.

"You said you wanted to act. I got you a script that's not shit. Either you're in or out. I can find someone to replace you," Donovan snapped. "Why? Got a better deal? Tell me who wants you. I'll up the offer."

He almost said he wasn't doing another film, but hell, if he could up the payout... "Double the offer and I might consider it."

"Two grand for one day's work? You're kidding me," Donovan blurted.

"Nope." Kris grinned to himself. He loved to dick Donovan over. He might be a nice guy, but he'd do what he needed to make the situation more profitable for himself.

"You're a douche." Donovan groaned. "I want to film tomorrow night so I've got the night sky as a backdrop. Would that work for you? I'll give you the two grand."

"Fine," Kris replied. Despite his windows being up and Donovan talking, he could hear the cries of the dog. His heart ached. The dog was an innocent and didn't deserve to be left outside again. Where was his neighbor?

"Good. I'll email you the script. Won't take you long to memorize it. Later." Donovan clicked off the line, leaving Kris in silence.

Kris tucked the phone into his front pocket. His neighbor parked in front of the condos and walked right past the dog. Despite the somewhat happy reaction from the canine—his tail wagged, even if he kept it between his legs—and he did creep toward Henry...the neighbor refused to give the dog any attention. No greeting, nothing. Kris climbed out of his car and grabbed the mail from the box. Something went flying out of the front door of his neighbor's condo and landed within feet of the dog.

What the fuck? He ran over to the chained dog. A thick soled boot lay in the dirt beside Nugent.

"Hey, Nugent." Kris held his hand out to the pit bull. "Hey, buddy." He allowed Nugent to sniff his hand, then he patted the dog's head. "What's the matter?"

"He's a fucking worthless dog, that's what." Henry stomped up to Kris. "I don't want him." Henry sneered. His forehead crinkled and the lines around his eyes deepened. Normally, he wasn't a bad looking guy, but the anger didn't improve his appearance.

"Why? What did he do to you?" Kris knelt beside the dog and continued to pet him. "He's a sweet boy."

"He belonged to that bitch I kicked out. She didn't want him and neither do I," Henry snapped.

"His ribs are showing. Did you feed him?" Kris asked. He rubbed the dog's belly. "He's starving." Christ. He should've intervened a long time ago.

"So?"

"You're an asshole. How much do you want for him? Give me his leash and anything else that's his. I'll take him. Got a dog license for him?" Kris unlocked the chain. "Cough it up."

"You're serious? I've got the papers inside. You can have him." Henry folded his arms. "Get him out of my sight. I might even pay you to get that piece of crap off my lawn."

Kris' fury hit the boiling point. He stood at his full height and glared at Henry. "From this moment on, he's mine and if I ever hear you call him crap or shit I will beat the *shit* out of you. No one messes with my dog." Kris patted his hip. "Come on, Nugent. We'll go home."

"Now you've got him, you're all high and mighty? You're a dickhead," Henry called.

Kris shook his head and ignored his shouting neighbor. Instead, he walked the dog to his condo, then unlocked the door. "Just don't pee on anything, big boy." He allowed the canine free rein of the house, then closed the door again. He kept his keys in his pocket and waited while his neighbor stomped across the lawn.

Henry plunked a dirty leash, a half-chewed plastic bowl and a ratty rope into Kris' hands. "That's all I got. Oh, and here's the license." He handed over a crumpled piece of paper. "He's all yours. Don't come crying to me when he shreds your shit or pisses everywhere."

"Have you ever thought maybe you were the problem?" Kris growled. "You treated him like dirt. He's a living thing and he's a good dog. I've never had an issue with him and he wasn't even mine."

"Well, he is now." Henry clapped his hands. "Out of my sight, out of my mind."

Kris rolled his eyes. The asshole. He headed back into the condo. Nugent sat on the hallway rug. The crying had stopped. He appeared to be a bit happier, but cautious as he stared at Kris.

"You're going to live with me now." Kris closed the door, then knelt next to the dog. "I'm going to take you in a bit in the car to get you a big bag of dog food and some other stuff. Do you like to ride in the car?"

The dog's eyes lit up and his tail wagged. Kris couldn't remember the last time he'd seen Nugent wag his tail without his tail being tucked between his legs.

"Good boy." He fastened the collar around Nugent's throat, then attached the leash. "Let's get you set up."

An hour later, he returned to the condo, loaded down with all the supplies needed for a dog. A gigantic pillow, flea shampoo, clippers, two bags of dog food, metal bowls for water and food, plus an array of toys.

"There." He allowed Nugent to run the condo again. He'd dropped more money than he'd wanted to on the supplies, but he'd saved the dog and gained company. Both were worth far more than actual cash.

His phone rang. Kris sighed. Who wanted him now? He didn't look at the screen before he answered. "No. I'm not doing another skin flick."

"Um…that's good because I wasn't going to ask about one," the caller said. "This is Zayn Mason. We spoke this afternoon about the Rock Magnus role."

"Oh my God. I'm so sorry." He slapped his hand over his mouth. *Fuck*. Of all the people to screw up in front of, his slip came when Zayn was listening. "I enjoyed the experience and hope I get to work with you."

"Well, that's partially why I called. I'd like you to come in tomorrow for another meeting. The producer, director and a couple members of the cast will be there. We'll also have a more informal audition over coffee. Sound like something you'd like to do?"

"Coffee with you?" Kris blurted. "You bet."

"It's not just with me," Zayn said. "The others will be there too. I go for the informal approach because I've learned I see how the cast will interact without the glare of the cameras. If the cast doesn't get along off-camera, they'll never work on screen." He laughed. "Make sense?"

"It does." Kris sat on the closest chair. "What time?"

"Ten a.m. Will that work for you?"

He sent up a quick prayer of thanks. "It will. Same building?"

"Yes."

Kris blew out a long breath. "I'll be there. Thank you for this opportunity."

"You're welcome. See you tomorrow," Zayn said, then hung up.

Kris sagged in his seat. A second audition. Either he'd really screwed up on the first or he'd impressed Zayn. A combination of excitement and fear gripped him. He was actually going out for a second audition. Holy shit. He'd get to see Zayn again. He frowned. But Zayn wouldn't be alone. Maybe he hadn't made such an impression on the casting director after all.

Oh well. The second audition. He wasn't completely out of the running for the part.

Nugent strolled up to him and bumped his hand. "Hey, Nuge." Kris sank to the floor and scratched the dog behind his ears. "Pretty cool, eh? A second audition. Are you my good luck charm?"

Nugent stared at him, then flopped onto the floor in front of him.

"You're one of the few decisions I don't regret." Kris scratched Nugent's belly. Of all the things he'd done, rescuing the dog was one of the better ones. Choosing to move to Los Angeles hadn't started his career off the way he'd expected. Getting into porn only sank his spirits. Sure, he owned a nice condo and a decent car, but he wasn't following his dream.

"If this role pans out, I won't have to do porn any longer," he said to the dog. "Like that?"

Nugent didn't answer, not that he expected anything like that from the dog.

"I do need to give you a bath. For all I know you've gotten fleas all over my condo. Do you like baths?" He clapped his hands. "Bath?"

Nugent sprang to his feet. His tail wagged and his tongue dangled down the side of his mouth. He bounded through the condo to the bathroom. Kris turned on the faucet. He coaxed the dog into the water, then little by little, bathed him. The mud, dirt and some fleas as well as some other debris washed out of Nugent's fur.

"Henry said you were a dangerous dog. He said you were worthless." Kris kissed the top of Nugent's now clean head. "He's a dick. You're a great dog." He toweled the canine off, then sent him running through the condo again. "Good thing you dry quickly," Kris said to the dog as he left the bathroom.

He rinsed the dirty water down the drain. His back ached from being hunched over, but at least he'd done something positive. Kris stood and stretched. He should jump in the shower.

Better check on the dog, first. He headed into the bedroom. Nugent lay sprawled out on the new dog bed pillow. Not asleep yet, but happily resting.

The LED light on Kris' phone flashed. A new text? Or email? He swiped his thumb across the screen. A new message from Donovan. He'd sent the script. Kris opened the document and scanned the pages. He wouldn't have to do much acting. Hell, the movie wasn't much more than a gigantic sex scene. A frat house picture, more or less. Donovan had made the thing out to be a whole lot more plot. But he'd been foolish enough to believe him.

Kris dragged his laptop and his phone into the bedroom, then stretched out on the mattress. Might as well get a jump on memorizing the script, such as it was. He read through his emails, then checked his stats on the Internet. His videos still garnered large numbers of hits.

"Too bad it's all for my naked ass," he mumbled.

Nugent stood, then crept over to the bed. Kris reached out to pet the dog. "You dry?" He scratched Nugent's head. "Sure are. Come on up." He patted the bed. "Keep me company."

Nugent stared at him for a moment, then crawled onto the mattress. He flopped beside Kris with his back touching Kris' leg.

"You're a cuddler, eh?" Kris continued to scratch the dog as he closed out of his email and the web browser, then pulled up the script document. "Mind if I read this to you?"

He knew the dog wasn't going to answer, but still. Having someone there to practice with was a nice change.

"Scene one — the meeting," Kris said. He and three other guys were to happen to run into each other in the lobby of the building and engage in small talk. One would be the boyfriend of another and Kris was there as the hunk they both wanted to fuck them. He rolled his eyes. As soon as he could get out of the business, he'd do it.

"You want a piece of this?" Kris gestured down his body. When the dog snorted, Kris nodded. "The script leaves a lot to be desired."

Honestly, there wasn't much to learn. Once they ended up in the bedroom, he was to tell the guys what to do. They'd first play around with each other so he could watch and then when he decided to jump in, he'd have them turn their attention to him.

Kris closed the laptop and placed it on his nightstand. After the audition and the situation with his neighbor, then the trip to the pet store, he'd used up the day. The moon lit up the sky.

"Somewhere under that moon is the guy who will understand me and what I want to do with my life." Kris plopped both hands onto his belly. "He wants me to succeed." He closed his eyes. Maybe he was more the romantic than he'd wanted to admit, but he truly believed there was someone out there for everyone. In his case, he hadn't found that guy yet.

His thoughts turned to Zayn, the casting director. There was a handsome guy. A guy with class and style. A guy who would never want to date another guy who did porn for a living.

But what if Zayn *were* interested? He'd never do a porno on camera with Zayn, but he'd sure love to act out one of the movies with him. His body heated at the thought. His skin prickled and he scooted down on the bed. He could almost see them together in his bedroom.

"Come here." Kris pointed to the doorway where Zayn stood. "You don't need to be over there all alone."

"No?" Zayn half-smiled. He'd shoved a hank of his sandy blond hair off his forehead. His deep-set blue eyes twinkled. "What should I be doing?"

"Letting me fuck you." Kris left the bed and walked across the room to Zayn. He pressed his lover into the doorframe and mashed their bodies together. "I've been dying to stick my cock in that ass all day."

Zayn shook his head. "No."

"No? You'd deny me?"

"I want you to make love to me."

Kris opened his eyes. *Just a fantasy.* No one actually wanted to make love anymore. Zayn might.

Kris glanced around his bedroom, then turned off the light. He might as well get something out of the fantasy then and keep going. He shoved both hands beneath the waistband of his boxer shorts and curled his fingers around his shaft. The elastic tightened around him. Damn it. He let go of his cock long enough to kick out of his underwear. Much better.

He stroked himself, but closed his eyes and pictured Zayn between his legs. A smile, a touch, a laugh…everything Zayn did turned him on. He slid one hand down to his balls and imagined Zayn licking him. Sweet Jesus. He loved when his partner sucked on his sac. The combination of tugging on his testicles and the sweet rhythm of a hand job turned his insides to mush. He chuckled and pumped his hips, thrusting into his hand.

"Fuck," Kris bit out. He squeezed his eyes shut tighter and gritted his teeth. The heat swirling through his body centered low in his belly. Everything within him tensed. He dug his feet into the mattress.

"That's much better," Zayn said, in the fantasy. "You're close to coming all over yourself."

"Want to come on you." Kris breathed hard. Almost there. Just a few more tugs. He increased the rhythm of his stroking until his resistance shattered. Cum spurted onto his belly in a hot ribbon. He sagged against the bed.

The dog, whom he'd forgotten was in the room, barked.

"Damn," Kris muttered. He grabbed his discarded underwear and cleaned up the mess, then turned his attention to the dog. "Sorry, buddy. Sorry."

Nugent quieted, then sat back down on the bed. Once Kris settled beneath the covers, the dog sprawled out on the foot of the mattress.

Kris tucked both hands behind his head. The fantasy was good and a great way to relieve the tension coiled within him, but fucking the casting director sure as hell wasn't going to get him a role. Even if it did, once the studio found out what he'd done, he'd end up being removed from the set. He wanted to be on the lot because of a real job there, not because he'd sucked the right dick or fucked the proper person. He wanted to be taken seriously for his craft and abilities. Someday.

Still, he could actually see himself spending time with Zayn. Odd, since he didn't know the guy and had pretty much a zero percent chance of getting to know him, but a guy could dream.

He allowed himself to drift to sleep, but thoughts of Zayn filled his dreams. He pictured them together in the condo. Rolling over to tell Zayn good night or asking him about the latest script he'd been given. They'd kiss before they turned the light off for the night and hold each other while they slept.

He opened his eyes. Either he was completely smitten with the casting director or losing his God damned mind. He'd practically built up a life for them already.

He didn't *know* the fucking casting director, yet he'd fallen a little in love with him. He needed to get out more. Needed a date or someone to get his mind off things he'd never have. He glanced at the clock. If he didn't get back to sleep, he'd never be ready for the second audition in the morning.

Fuck. The second audition. He'd have to face Zayn and not act like a doofus. All the horny thoughts would come back and he'd blow his chances. Why? Because he'd fantasized about the casting director. He scrubbed both hands over his face and groaned. He was so screwed.

"Hi," he murmured to himself. "I'm Kris Hunter. I'm here to read, for a second time, for the role of Rock. I've got the script memorized, but I need the casting director to step out while I go through this. Why? Oh, I've got a Texas-sized crush on him and I've been thinking dirty thoughts about him since last night. It's nothing, but I won't be able to focus if he's watching. Do you mind?"

He snorted. Like anyone—even he—would buy that. Kris stared at Nugent's sleeping form. If he wanted to get out of the porn industry and become the real actor he knew he could be, then he'd have to get his head out of the clouds and into the script. His passion was great, but not going to get him anywhere if he couldn't focus.

"I will shine," he told himself. "I will."

Now if he just believed himself, he'd be golden.

* * * *

Kris climbed out of bed and showered. If he wanted to nab the part of Rock, he needed to be the character. He stood before his closet and rummaged through the different outfits. Rock's taste ran more in the tight fashion—garments that showed off his muscles. As if his attitude wasn't enough, he presented the tough guy exterior to back everything up.

Kris picked out one of his favorite and nearly threadbare T-shirts. The soft cotton clung to him like a second skin. He stepped into a pair of briefs, then one of his butter-soft pairs of ratty jeans. With a thick belt and gigantic buckle, he actually could've been a badass—could've. Too bad he didn't believe the image he presented. He might be the top in his relationships, but he was no badass. He followed the rules and stayed in line—except for the porn thing and his normally out-of-control dating life. Those were the only two places he played in the gray areas. He liked to date a lot and usually not the same guy twice. Then there was his choice of jobs. Maybe he and Rock had more in common than he'd thought.

He put his socks on, then stepped into his thick motorcycle boots. Add his leather jacket and the one heavy gold chain he owned and he should be set. He adjusted the collar on the jacket, then donned a pair of sunglasses.

"What do you think?" he asked Nugent.

The dog flopped onto his side at Kris' feet.

"Guess that's a vote of confidence. Gotta go outside before I leave?" He patted his hip. He let the dog out and waited until he'd done his business, then brought Nugent back in. "You've got your food, toys, your bed and my bed and wherever else you want to sleep. Don't eat me out of house and home. Okay? I'll be back in an hour or two, tops." He patted Nugent's head. "Guard the house and don't let any bad guys in."

He picked up his keys, phone, wallet and the script. He locked the condo, then headed across town to the studio. His heart lodged in his throat when he pulled into the parking lot. This was his chance. A plum role that practically screamed his name and he could do it. He could pull off Rock. He'd have to deal with some of the demons from his past, but he could handle the emotional issues.

He parked, then headed into the building. The receptionist smiled and pointed him toward the correct meeting room. He smiled back. The last time he'd been to the studio, another woman had sat behind the round counter.

"Sir?" the receptionist called.

Kris stopped. *Oh shit.* "Yes?" All he needed was for her or anyone else to recognize him and not for his prior visit.

"You need this badge." She hurried up to him and handed him a clip-on plastic card. "Then if the security stops you, they know you're supposed to be here." She smiled, but didn't walk away. "You look familiar."

"I've been told that. I guess I've got that kind of face," he said. The longer he stood with her, the better his chances of being found out.

"No, I think I've seen you before. Were you here to audition for another role?" She clasped her hands together. "That's got to be it. I hope you get the role." She glanced down the hallway, then plunked something else into his palm before she strode away.

He waited until he rounded the corner to read the paper. She'd given him her phone number. Hell. Of all the things he'd expected, getting the receptionist's number wasn't one of them. He slipped the paper into his pocket. Maybe he could use the new item to his advantage in the audition.

Kris sat outside the boardroom with three other actors. He'd seen all three before. One guy made a career out of starring in commercials. He'd been the

Zippy paper towel guy, the Burns antacid heartburn sufferer and the Tots candy maker. The second guy had a recurring role on a television show, but never quite reached star status. The third man glanced over at Kris and nodded. Patterson Bryce. He'd be the one to give Kris a run for his acting money.

Kris bit back his uneasiness. He knew he'd have to go up against actors with more experience and savvy, but Patterson Bryce? Hell. The guy could've bought the role if he'd wanted it that bad.

He wasn't going to leave. Hell no. He'd worked to garner a second audition and refused to walk out early.

"They're down to the final four, I hear," Patterson said. "The four of us."

"I see," Kris replied. He wasn't sure why Patterson wanted to chat. Normally, Patterson was given special treatment. If he was out in the hallway with the others, then maybe he wasn't really right for the role after all. Or the producers and directors wanted to humble him. Kris snorted to himself. Patterson needed a bit of humbling.

"They'll see right through you. This isn't for the minor leaguers. It's not even for the faint of heart. This is the big time. A major motion picture." Patterson folded his arms. "I see you've dressed for the part. Think that's going to give you a leg up?"

"Might." Shit. He'd gone overboard with the outfit. No, he was going with the projected confidence. *You are what you want to be.* Couldn't hurt. "You never know."

"It won't. It's crap. They'll see right through your shtick—and that's all it is…shtick." Patterson laughed. "But good luck. If they're interested in a current porn star, then they might take anyone."

The door opened and a young man, in his early twenties, waved to Patterson. "Next."

"Looks like they want the best man for the job. This isn't your league, Hunter. Go home." Patterson snorted. "But since you're staying, good luck." He waved, then headed into the room.

Kris bit back a groan and forced himself to remain calm. Giving in to Patterson's teases wasn't going to help. He needed to act like Rock and run with the character's nuances. He was an actor, clothes on or off. He could do this role if given the chance. He'd like for the producers and directors to see beyond his current job, but beggars couldn't be choosers.

"Don't listen to him. He's pissed that they made him come back."

Kris glanced up at the speaker. Zayn.

Zayn waved his fingers. "I need you."

"Right now?" He glanced over at the other two guys waiting for their audition times. "Me?" God, he sounded so silly.

"Yeah. Come here." Zayn grinned. "Now."

He might have been a top, but he did know how to take commands. Kris scurried to his feet and strode over to Zayn. "Yes. I'm here. I dressed for the part. Too much, probably." He needed to shut up.

"I like it." Zayn's gaze swept over Kris. "It's great. I'm making note of it for Carla. She'll love your attention to detail."

As he stood before Zayn, realization washed over Kris. Fuck. If he was being called aside, this wasn't a good thing. They were going to tell him to get moving and not come back. He shouldn't be so negative, but he'd been down this road before—fifty-one times to be exact.

"Okay, so here's the deal. We've got Patterson in there right now. I want you to go around to the back entrance. It's just down the hallway and to the left. Do that so he doesn't see you coming or going. I'll be honest. You're the best competition he's got and I'm tired of his diva shit." Zayn put his hand up, almost touching Kris' chest, then stopping. "Yeah?"

"I can do that." He wasn't being told to go home. "Right now? Or wait? I don't want to do the wrong thing."

"Right now. He'll be done in a little bit and I'm sure he'll pitch a fit. He knows I left, so he's probably figured out something's up." Zayn grinned. His eyes sparkled. "Cool?"

"Cool." Kris nodded, then turned on his heel. Down the hallway, then to the left. He followed the directions to the correct door. Instead of yanking the handle, he paused. Through the thick wood of the barrier, he could hear Patterson running through the lines. He winced. Patterson had a gruffer delivery.

"He sounds too mad," Kris muttered. He rolled his eyes. The character of Rock was supposed to be smooth and on the verge of scary. The rest of the characters were afraid of him because they could never be sure if he was angry, revenge-filled or happy. Would he come apart and freak out or stay level and calm? Patterson either hadn't studied the character or the script or he had his own idea for how to deliver the lines. Being overly tough and nasty might be Patterson's go-to character, but it wasn't Rock.

You've got to follow the character arc. You can't make him something he's not because it's your thing. From his years in porn, Kris had learned how to have a persona, but also how to listen to the nuances of the character being played. Every person in porn wasn't a Dominant, just as every porn star wasn't sex-crazed and trying to get laid.

The longer he listened, the more his confidence boosted. He didn't have the part locked down, but if Zayn was right and he was the other major contender, then he had a pretty good shot. He liked his odds.

He closed his eyes and sent up a small prayer. "Please God, don't let me screw this up. Help me to follow my passion and do what I'm meant to be doing." He leaned against the wall and waited quietly for the signal. He could do this. He could nail this part and become the actor he'd always longed to be.

Chapter Three

Zayn sat in the audition room and twiddled with his phone. He'd had to listen to Patterson for more than twenty minutes. Christ. The guy wasn't getting the gist of the role. Rock was tough, but not a complete dick. To hear Patterson's interpretation, the character would never charm his way into a woman's bed. No freaking way. To hear Myron talk, Patterson was the answer to their prayers. Patterson was the actor they needed. Myron was a jerk and completely wrong.

Instead of paying attention to the awful audition, Zayn turned the sound down on his phone. He tapped the Internet icon and brought up the search engine. He typed in Kris' name again and hoped for better results.

"Whoa," he murmured. Of all the videos, there weren't any non-porn ones.

"What?" Jordan muttered. "Tell me it's better than this."

Zayn elbowed the director and showed him the screen. Without the sound, he had no idea what was actually being said, but the actions were crystal clear. "It's not kink, but it's definitely porn."

Jordan slid his notepad over to Zayn. *You wouldn't know,* he wrote. *You haven't had sex in forever.*

Bastard. Zayn lifted his middle finger, flipping his friend off.

What happened to your last boyfriend? Eli? Jordan wrote.

Before Zayn could answer, Patterson finished the reading. Myron stood, applauding. "Let's take a break." He continued to clap and turned his attention to Patterson. "Give us some time to discuss the results, but I'm sure you'll be hearing from us soon."

Patterson smiled, his eyes narrowed, then walked out of the room with Myron at his side.

"Nothing says favorites like having the producer in your back pocket." Jordan elbowed Zayn. "So, your boy is in porn. No question. Eli started doing that, too, didn't he?"

"Last I knew, he was doing skin flicks. I didn't get him the results he wanted in Hollywood and since he refused to work on getting himself an actual acting job, he left. I haven't checked on him or even heard from him in more than two years." Zayn stretched and cracked his back. "I don't want to hear from him."

"Okay, follow me on this," Jordan said. "How do you know this one will be any different?"

"Who? Kris?" Zayn frowned. "I don't—wait." Realization washed over him. "Don't you dare get any ideas. This is strictly professional."

"You went out there to talk to him. That's not professional. That's you trying to get a date without admitting to anyone that you actually want a date." Jordan chuckled. "You know he's not going to get the part. We can have him read from now until hell freezes over, but Myron's not moving. He wants Patterson."

"I know."

"So what are you going to do if you hook up with this guy and he turns out to be a mirror image of Eli?" Jordan asked.

"He won't."

"You're sure?"

Zayn folded his arms. "I am. I'm not going to let things with Kris get that far. We're not going to date or get that close."

"Good luck." Jordan shook his head and left the table. "Call me when we're ready to jerk that poor guy's chain and fuck him over. I don't want to do it, but I can't stop Myron."

Zayn stared at the mangled script and thought about Kris. He couldn't help but be a little eager for Kris to come in. When he'd called Kris the day before, he sounded buoyed. Having to tell the actor that they simply wanted him for an audition deflated his happiness a bit. Zayn liked the way they seemed to get along and although he wasn't planning on getting close to Kris, he wanted to work with him.

He should be more cautious, but he didn't get the usual 'cocky bastard actor' vibe from Kris. Maybe Kris wanted to fuck his way up the ladder to a dream part in a big movie, but if he did, he'd get the biggest wake-up call of his life.

Across the room, Kris opened the door. He waited by the doorway, but didn't approach. Zayn got a better look at him. He'd seen him for the few moments in the hall, but in the better light, he loved what he saw. The tight T-shirt and threadbare jeans clung to his muscled frame, showcasing the strength of his body. The jacket gave the air of toughness, but wasn't over the top. He clomped across the room in thick motorcycle boots and had slicked his hair off his forehead. The man personified handsome, but dangerous and beguiling.

As far as Zayn was concerned, Kris was Rock.

Myron, Jordan and the other actors filed into the room. "Who is this?" Myron barked. "Are you the next audition?"

"I'm Kris Hunter," Kris said. He extended his hand. "Thank you for this chance."

Myron glared at Zayn.

"What?" Zayn asked. He wasn't going to be bullied by Myron. "As you can see, he fits the physical description for the part. Let him read. You'll see."

Kris dropped his hands to his sides. All the confidence he'd showcased a moment before evaporated. He shrank back a bit from the table. "I overdid the costume. Sorry." The tips of his ears and the apples of his cheeks reddened.

"Yes, it is," Myron crabbed. "No one does that."

"You're fine," Zayn said. "I love it. I made notes."

Myron grabbed Zayn's shoulder. He didn't take his glare off Kris. "Zayn? A word?" He yanked Zayn out of his seat and toward the door. Without leaving the room, Myron unleashed his fury. He kept his voice low, but not quiet enough to prevent everyone in the room from hearing. "What the fuck? He's in porn. I've seen his body of work—and his body. I refuse to put that sick fuck in my film. There is award buzz around this picture. He'll kill that buzz and only draw people wanting to see the freak, not the actual film."

"Have you seen him act?"

"I don't need to. I've seen *his* act. He strips and fucks...a lot." Myron pinned Zayn in the doorway. "You're pulling shit again."

"God. You always think that. You sound like my damn father and even *he* wasn't this much of a prick." Zayn massaged his temples. "Jesus. I've seen Kris Hunter act. He's good. He might be a wild card, but he's what we need. He's got the rawness and intensity to pull off Rock without turning him into a caricature. He'll kill the part and get you the awards you're so desperate to grab."

"You're right on one account. He's going to kill something…my movie. No one wants to see a porn star in a regular film. Passion, desire, whatever the fuck you want to call it, he doesn't have it." Myron's eyes narrowed. "Name me one porn star who has crossed over successfully."

"You have no faith in him or me."

"You can't do it." Myron's voice dropped to a whisper. "I'll pull funding and then you'll have your buddy, Jordan, kicking your ass. Do you want that? No you don't."

Zayn forked his fingers into his hair. Too much rode on his decision, but damn it, he believed in Kris. "No, I can't name a porn star that crossed over. Most of them don't want to." He dropped his voice to a growl. "You need to give him a chance. What if he's the wild card that will make this picture shine? You won't know if you boot him."

"I'm not going to waste his time." Myron turned around and strode up to Kris. His voice went from venom-filled to sugary sweet. "I'm going to save you the hassle of reading this script. Why? Because time is money. I know what I want on this picture and you're not him. We're going in the direction of Patterson. Thank you for your time."

Myron walked away from Kris and the rest of the actors.

"Thank you," Kris said. He held his head high and marched past Zayn, right out of the room.

Zayn caught a whiff of Kris' cologne. The woodsy scent lingered in his nose. Of all the things to notice…cologne. Zayn watched Kris make his way into the foyer, then out of the building. *Fuck.*

"That worked so well." Jordan rolled his eyes. "I swear. Myron, if you're set on Patterson, then fine. I can't do this without your patronage. Zayn, I'm sorry. I've got to go where the money is." He clapped his friend on the back, then left.

Zayn debated punching something, but didn't follow through. Why waste the energy on breaking something, probably his own hand? He grabbed his phone and tablet from the table, then ran through the building. He needed to find Kris.

In the parking lot, Zayn stopped. God damn it. He didn't know what kind of car Kris drove. He'd waited too long to hunt the actor down. Shit. He groaned and scanned the lot. Maybe, just maybe Kris hadn't gone.

A black car pulled up beside Zayn and stopped. The window rolled down. "Hey, thanks for the chance."

Zayn tilted his head to see the driver. Kris. "Hi."

"I appreciate you saying something to the director, but I get it."

"No, I don't think you do." Zayn gripped the window frame of the car. "That was bullshit. He's a dumb ass for overlooking you."

"He did me a favor." Kris shrugged. "He was right. I've got the desire, but I made a major mistake. I should've stuck to waiting tables like everyone else. But seriously, thank you. I learned a lot."

He drummed his fingers on the frame. "Do you have a few moments? Pull over into the visitor spots. Please?"

"I'm not a charity case." Kris shook his head. "Thanks, but you've done enough."

"I haven't done anything—yet." He held up both hands. "Look, I saw something in your performance.

You had the part of Rock nailed. The other actors haven't shown that kind of spark."

"But you think I did?" Kris slapped the steering wheel. "You embarrassed me. I know I'm not the best actor or the most handsome, but I felt like an idiot in there."

"I'm sorry." God, he'd screwed up.

"Yeah, well, sorry isn't enough."

"I know." He needed to say something intelligent and convincing to get Kris to stick around. He needed a little longer with him in order to bring out the brilliance he saw lurking underneath Kris' porn star exterior.

"Myron Bixby is gunning for me. I've auditioned for him four times now and every time he has some excuse why I can't work for him. I'm getting the hint. Porn equals bad person." He sighed. "Yes, I'm doing porn. Yes, it pays the bills. No, I'm not entirely proud, but it's keeping me and my dog in food and a shelter."

"You've got a dog?" Zayn blurted. He'd cooked up an idea that all porn stars lived in the nude and had sex all the time.

"Is that a problem?" Kris snapped. "I don't know why I'm still talking to you. I should've known. Jumping out of the adult industry and into the mainstream is tricky. I'm not cut out for it." He offered his hand. "Thank you for your time and the lessons learned. I've got to get home."

"Wait. I brought you back because I wanted to see if you could show me that spark again. I never got the chance to see what you've rehearsed," Zayn said. "You were good. *Damn* good. I've got actors taking classes trying to be what you were. Give me a chance to prove to you that you do have what it takes to be a mainstream actor." He'd seen plenty of actors who wanted to be good. Actors who tried to capture the intensity they needed for the role. Whatever the reason, Kris just had something about him.

"Why? So you can feel better about yourself?"

Kris sounded ungrateful, but Zayn noticed the glimmer of hope in his eyes. The attitude was a shield. He'd probably been turned down so much that his pride was shot to hell.

"This isn't about me. This is about a guy with a gift who needs to find the right movie in order to show the world he's a diamond." He'd resorted to pleading, but he didn't care.

"Wow." Kris stared straight ahead. "You really see all that?"

"I do. Now please pull over into the visitor lot. We *really* need to talk." Zayn held his breath. He'd really put himself out there and hoped Kris wouldn't run his ass over.

Kris flexed his hands on the steering wheel, then rolled forward into the closest parking spot. When he stopped, he unlocked the doors.

Zayn glanced back at the building before he jumped into Kris' car. "I know. I'm not the person you want to be around right now. But you need to understand something. I tried to change Myron's mind. I did."

"He's convinced. I get it. I'm a freak." Kris didn't look at him. "He's right. I am. I'm trying to jump from one bad situation into another where I'll have to put all my shit on the table. Everything I've done will be fodder for whoever wants to smear my ass."

Zayn frowned. Although he wouldn't have put the description quite the same way, he understood what Kris meant. "You're under the magnifying glass and every screw up will grab attention."

"Yeah."

"Then let's not screw up any longer."

"Let's?" Kris twisted around in his seat. "Where are you getting let's out of what I said?"

"I've got a plan." Zayn nodded. Five minutes before, he wasn't sure what he was going to do. That morning, his life had all been planned out. A little spontaneity sounded good. "First, you want out of porn, right?"

"I do, but I've got one more picture tonight."

"Oh." Zayn nodded again. He could work with this. "Let me come along."

"To the shoot?"

"Yes." Zayn tapped the pages on his tablet. "Okay. Now, you want out of porn. I can help you. First, we get you into some independent films. Build up your credibility. Once you've got enough of those under your belt, you can stop using the porn films on your résumé. Let the independent work show what you can do. If you're asked about the porn, then yeah, it's there, but don't advertise."

"You're serious?"

"I am. I've been in the movie business my entire life. Please, let me do this." Zayn grabbed Kris' hand. "I can help you."

Kris sighed. He didn't say anything right away. Instead he continued to flex his free hand on the steering wheel. "When do you want to get started? Tonight?"

"Yes." Without a doubt. He was crazy, but working with Kris meant they'd be spending time together. He'd get to know the actor better and could help promote him properly. They'd have to be around each other and if something happened romantically...he might not push Kris away.

"Fine, but I'll warn you. You'll have to say you're my agent or something because Donovan will try to con you into doing part of the scene with me." Kris offered his hand. "Thanks."

"Then I'm your agent—of sorts. You said you had to feed the dog. Why don't I follow you? I've got my car and I don't want to leave it here on the lot. You can show me your portfolio and we can get started. Yes?"

"Yeah." Kris nodded. For the first time since he'd walked into the studio building, Kris smiled, but it wasn't a fake smile. The happiness lit in his eyes. "I'm over in the Hillshire development."

"Nice. I've got the Jaguar. I'll tail you." He shook hands with Kris, then left the vehicle. Although he'd done a crazy thing by more or less leaving the studio in order to help one particular actor, he felt lighter. A weight had been lifted from his shoulders. He bounded over to his sports car, then zipped up to Kris as he exited the lot.

Zayn laughed until his chest hurt. He'd left the studio. Christ, he was crazy. The studios paid his bills. If he was truly going to see things through with Kris, he'd have to pick up some more work on major motion pictures. The indie flicks didn't pay much. But he was free—for now. He pressed the buttons on the dash. Time to make some phone calls. He knew plenty of directors who were always in the midst of making some sort of independent film. Most of them hired friends or cheap actors for the pictures. Maybe he could line up a few interviews and auditions for Kris.

He dialed his buddy, Paul. He'd known Paul since high school. Of their circle of friends, Paul was the only one to follow his dream and direct movies. The rest either still worked as wait staff or had moved on to other careers.

After three rings, Paul answered. "How the hell are you, Z? You're calling me. What's wrong? Did you get married or are you trying to get into a movie?"

"Remember telling me you had a dick for a leading man and you wanted a change?" Zayn asked. "I might have your answer."

"He has to be sexy. I can't have a fugly guy for my girlfriend to hang on." Paul laughed. "But seriously, you got someone in mind?"

"Do you have the script on the computer?"

"Always," Paul replied.

"Good. Send me a copy. I've got a guy who should be just right—if he's willing to do a gore-fest." Zayn tapped the steering wheel. "He's new, but he's good. Solid."

"Is he your boyfriend? I don't want any messy shit when you split."

"You always say that, but you're the one who dates your leading ladies. God. But no, I'm not dating him." *Yet.* Zayn snorted. He wasn't sure where that thought had come from. He wasn't going date Kris. No way.

"Good. Don't," Paul said. "I'll send this script over today. Get back to me like soon because I want to get the costuming shots done and get rolling. Shouldn't take more than a few weeks and the pay won't be great, but if he's wanting experience and another line for his résumé, I might be able to use him."

"I'll let him know. Thanks." Zayn hung up on his friend. "Fuck yeah." He loved his job as a casting director. The idea of hunting through tons of actors just to find the right one for the part was exciting. Like a treasure trip each time. But this agent business…he'd never thought about putting his contacts into use. He turned onto a side street and followed Kris down a winding road to a gated community.

"Never would've pictured him living here," he said to himself. The condos all looked the same, but each lawn featured a little something different—be it a statue or flowers or a tree. He pulled up behind Kris' car and glanced over at the condo to the right. In the middle of the otherwise manicured lawn was a wide circle of bare earth.

"What happened there?" Zayn asked as he exited his car. He nodded to the adjacent lawn, then pressed the fob to lock the vehicle.

"That's where my dog lived." Kris waved him forward. "I'll explain later. For now, let me get a few things straightened out. Not every porn actor or actress lives in filth. We take care of ourselves because if we're sick or have something hinky happening, we can't work. In addition, this is my house. I paid for it and other than the dog, it's my prized possession. I'm tired of apartments and living with other people. I needed my own space. Concerning the dog, Nugent was left outside and neglected for a long time. I rescued him, but I have no idea how he'll react to strangers. He's always been good for me, but you're new. Offer your hand and allow him to make the first move. Should be fine, but, just in case. Okay?"

"Good deal." Zayn stole another glance at the circle of dirt. Who left their dog outside all the time? California had pretty decent weather, but still. He waited for Kris to open the door. The dog bounded up to them. When the canine spotted Zayn, he backed away.

"Hey, buddy." Kris stepped into the condo, then knelt next to the dog. "It's okay. It's me." He cuddled Nugent. "Big boy. Did you have a good time alone in the condo? I don't see any torn up stuff." He glanced back at Zayn. "Nuge, this is my friend, Zayn. He's a good guy. He won't hurt you. Don't eat him."

Zayn dropped to his knees next to Kris and offered the back of his hand. "Hi, Nugent. You're a big boy, aren't you? A good boy?"

The dog eyed him warily, then sniffed Zayn's hand. No growl or any other noise, but he didn't warm right up to Zayn, either.

"I like you, Nugent. You're a sweet dog." From the animal's demeanor, he could tell the critter had been abused, but loved his rescuer, Kris. *Lucky dog.* Christ. Another random thought that wasn't important. Well, no, it was important. He wanted to be loved by someone too. An unconditional love by a guy he could come home to and snuggle with at night.

"You still in there?" Kris waved his hand in front of Zayn's face. "You're a million miles away."

"Sorry." Zayn blinked. He'd spaced out? Shit. "Didn't want to make any sudden moves and freak out the dog."

"It's cool. He won't come right up to you, but he's not growling, so it should be fine." Kris shrugged. "He had it pretty rough."

"You said you'd explain. What happened?" Zayn allowed the dog to sniff his hand again. Slowly, Nugent crept up to him and butted his head against Zayn's palm.

"Long story short, the asshole next door had a girlfriend who brought home a dog—Nugent. I have no idea where she or he got the name, if it was a football player or the musician. Anyway, she never paid the dog much attention and when she left—or was kicked out, I'm never sure over there—the asshole ignored Nugent. I'd take him food and water because I felt sorry for him. I kind of understood. He was in a situation he had no control over. Guess I'm a sucker for animals too."

"I think it's very cool that you rescued him." Zayn petted the dog and watched Kris move around the room. The man had grace. His actions seemed so calculated but easy. His condo spoke volumes about him too. A place for everything and everything in its place. No photos on the wall or art, instead a gigantic mirror decorated the wall above the sofa. If Zayn didn't know better, he'd have thought Kris rented the place.

"When did you get the condo? Gated communities around here are hard to get into." Zayn stood, then joined Kris at the dining table. Two chairs, just enough for a plus one. He touched the back of the second chair. "May I?"

"Sit, sure." Kris crinkled his eyebrows a second, then shook his head. "I know. I've heard all the lines. Porn stars must be self-absorbed and a thousand other horrible things. It's not true — well, not entirely. There are some who really need to clean up their acts, but that's their problem."

"You're really defensive." Zayn sat opposite Kris. "I meant, I like the condo and wanted to get one in a gated community. I'd like to get the name of the owner."

"Oh." Kris half-smiled. "Sorry. I've dealt with a lot of crap lately."

"Like?"

"Nothing that concerns you."

"Okay." Zayn folded his arms. "I'm going to be blunt. I don't like bullshit and I will call you on the carpet. I'm here to help you. I need some background so I can do my job properly. If you get all moody on me, then I can't. So, if you want in the movies, you'll open your damn mouth."

Kris' eyes widened. He probably hadn't had anyone talk to him in such a terse tone in a long time. "I'll level with you. Fifty-one times I've gone up for roles. Not just movie roles. I'm talking commercials for cough syrup and cereal. I even went out for a local commercial for a realtor. I was supposed to be house hunting with my wife—har, har—and that didn't even pan out. The guy said I didn't have the right look. I pulled out every stop. I wore very conservative clothes, left my earring out and kept my hair natural. It wasn't enough."

"Then show me your résumé. You've got it on the computer, right?"

"Just a moment." Kris left the table and disappeared down the short hallway.

Zayn dropped his hands into his lap. Although there was a combativeness to Kris, the banter came easily too. Kris almost seemed to want someone to talk to, even if he wasn't ready to admit that fact to himself. He glanced around the condo again. All the little touches that should've been there to make the place a home, not just a dwelling, weren't there. The living room put Zayn to mind of someone who was trying so hard to be something else that he lost himself. Probably silly to assume such things about Kris. But he managed to keep a sturdy façade going and said exactly what was on his mind. Both qualities endeared him to Zayn.

"Here. I copied the file so if you want to make changes, do it on this document." Kris moved the chair beside Zayn. "I'm trusting you."

"I won't let you down." Zayn turned the computer enough that they both could read the screen. He scanned the words, but didn't really read them. "I need to ask. What is your driving reason for getting out of porn? I'd love to know how you got into it, but first, why do you want out?"

Kris crossed his ankles, then folded his arms again. He bobbed his head back and forth, then sighed. "I came to California because I had this crazy dream in high school that I was going to be the next leading man. I was going to take Hollywood by storm. Stupid, looking back. I was so young and dumb. I had no idea what I was getting into." He stared at Zayn. "You know how many guys come out here every day thinking they're going to make the big time."

Zayn nodded. More than he could count and almost all of them ended up either waiting tables or heading back home.

"I couldn't go home, so I waited tables over at Maggio's. The money wasn't bad, but it wasn't great. Well, one day one of the servers comes in and he asks me if I'm gay. I was brash and told the truth. Nothing to be ashamed of. Says if I like to fuck and want to on camera, I can make twice the money per night. I heard 'camera' and 'fuck' and signed on that night. The one director said I had a presence on film. He called me back plenty of times and I made a lot of flicks. At one point I was up for a super fuck award or something like that. I never checked to see if I won. Anyway, the more of those movies I made, the more that light within me died. I've never been high on myself, but I kept getting lower and lower. About a year ago, I decided come hell or high water, I was getting out. The passion isn't there any longer—not that it ever really was. I want to do more than show my ass off to whoever happens to click that link."

Zayn leaned back in his chair. He hadn't been sure how he felt about Kris up to that moment. Yes, he was attracted to the man, but who wasn't? He was handsome. But hearing Kris' truths, he respected him. That and the bullshit meter hadn't gone off.

"How do you feel about horror movies?" Zayn asked. "I know, totally off-topic, but I was given a tip. I'm setting up an audition for you — if you want to go for it. He's sending me the script tonight."

"I'm confused."

"I've got a friend making independent films. Right now, he's working on a horror flick. He's sending me the script for you to read. I'll go over it with you and if you're interested in becoming a horror movie actor for at least one film, it's one film closer to bettering your cred in Hollywood." Zayn put both hands in the air. "I know. I get it. You've been used by the porn industry. You want out and should be out. I see that fire in you. Horror films are fun. It's acting and unless you want to, you don't have to show your ass. It'll help you see that your bone-deep need to act is still there." He'd leaned closer to Kris. Although he shouldn't, he wanted to kiss him.

Kris' breath warmed Zayn's cheeks. "I've got the other film to do tonight," he murmured. "Porn, again."

"You've got some time. It's not like he's going to want an answer right now." Partially a lie, but he didn't care. Zayn wanted to reach for Kris. Odd, since they barely knew each other, but he did. The draw to Kris was strong. He understood exactly why porn wanted Kris. The guy was hot and had a heart. The innocence in his eyes hadn't gone away, just dimmed a bit.

Kris nodded. "Okay. I'll give it a shot."

"Yeah?" He barely recognized the gravelly tone of his own voice.

"I'm done with porn," Kris said. "Meaning you're going to have to seriously act as my agent. Want to come along with me to a porn shoot?"

He was a cad. A total dick because he completely wanted to visit the shoot with Kris. The opportunity to see the handsome man in the nude was too much to pass up. He licked his lips. "Yeah, I do."

Chapter Four

Kris wanted to back away. He shouldn't be so close to Zayn. For God's sake, Zayn was almost Hollywood royalty and he wasn't much above sewer level. He balled his fists to keep from grabbing the front of Zayn's shirt to pull him in for a kiss.

"I need to get ready for the shoot," Kris said. He needed to say something to break the tension between them. "My stuff..."

"Okay." Zayn closed the lid of the laptop. "Do what you need to. I'll be right here waiting."

What a loaded couple of statements. Kris dragged a breath into his lungs and eased away from Zayn. His heart hammered. He hadn't felt so much like wanting to fuck someone else in a long time. Sex had become a job, not exciting or fun. He pushed away from the chair and headed down the hallway. A thought occurred to him. He'd forgotten what he needed for the call that night.

"Can you grab my computer? I need it for few moments," Kris called. He picked up his favorite black bag. Nugent trotted into the room and hopped onto the bed. "Gotta get ready," he said to the canine.

"What?" Zayn strolled into the bedroom with the laptop in hand. "I see the king has his spot."

"He's assumed his place on the bed, yeah." Kris opened the computer and scrolled through his email for the one from Donovan.

"What is your prep for one of these films?" Zayn leaned against the wall.

"Well...first, I have to find out what's needed. If I'm supposed to wear something in particular or anything. Some situations require special clothing—like leather gear or uniforms." He slid his gaze over Zayn. He'd love to see Zayn in nothing but a pair of tight leather pants and shitkicker boots...or even a pair of tight jeans and nothing else. Speaking of nothing but jeans, he wanted to see Zayn sporting that style. He shivered. He shouldn't be thinking about Zayn in any sexual way. Things weren't going to happen between them. "Anyway, I never wear the costume to the actual shoot. It's always in my bag. I take stock of the other stuff I need. Like this is a straight ménage film. Three guys fucking. I play a voyeur." The tips of his ears burned. "I've got rules when I perform. I never get fucked and I always use condoms. If there's a ménage, I'm on top."

"Smart," Zayn said. He picked up the box. "I like a guy who thinks ahead. Not everyone does."

"I bring condoms because you'd be surprised how many shoots don't have them. Lube, and an extra set of clothes for the ride home." He pulled up the email to deter his thoughts from getting sexual again. "Okay, so Donovan wants me in jeans, sans underwear, and a necktie. What the hell?"

Zayn chuckled. "I bet you look hot in that getup."

"Maybe, but why in the hell would I be wearing nothing but jeans, boots and a tie so I can watch two other guys fuck? What is my job supposed to be?"

"Handsome male escort coming home from a rowdy night with the guys?" Zayn chuckled. "Sorry, but I could see it."

I'm sure you can, Kris thought. He'd been in so damn many movies that pretty much any outfit and job was possible. He rubbed his face, then shook his head. He'd done too many movies, plain and simple. Once the flick was over, he was done. "You're going to be there to tell Donovan to fuck himself, right? I can say it all day long, but he won't buy it from me. You're new."

"I've got powers of persuasion." Zayn smiled. "You'll be fine." He sat on the bed and folded the pair of jeans. Once finished, he handed the garment to Kris. "I doubt he'll be interested in me."

"I know I will be fine, but I'm starting to worry about you." Kris grabbed a navy necktie from the closet. "I've been in this business for six years. I've seen fresh-faced boys go from sweethearts to dicks in a matter of months. Donovan will either hate you because you come off as a hard ass or he'll love you and try to con you into doing the films." He'd seen plenty of friends capitulate to the idea of making lots of money just for having sex. "He'll look at you and his next thought will be how to get you to drop your damn pants."

"You forget. My father was big in Hollywood. I learned at a young age to hold my own. It didn't work with Myron, but the man's a jackass. Donovan sounds like another jackass. I know what battles to fight and this is one that needs another hero."

Kris frowned. He tossed the second box of condoms and another bottle of lube into the bag. "Another hero? Who's the first?"

"You." Zayn left the wall and stood beside Kris. He placed his hand on Kris' on the duffle. "Getting into that business is easy. Getting out is the hard part. You've got the drive to get out and the need to act. I'm not letting that fire go out."

Kris leaned into Zayn and pressed a kiss to his lips. He shouldn't have. They were going to have a working relationship, not a sexual one, but damn. Resisting the temptation would kill him. The kiss didn't last long, but the connection seared Kris to the core.

"Whoa." Zayn pulled away first. He touched his lips. "We—we can't do that."

"I know." Kris dipped his head and picked up both the bag and his computer. He'd screwed up royally. God. Zayn wasn't interested in him. He'd imagined the attraction. *Fucking balls.* He cleared his throat. "The next thing I do is go over the lines I'm supposed to have and since I've got Nugent here, he's my partner."

"I'll help." Zayn touched Kris' arm. "I want to." The pity in Zayn's eyes unnerved Kris.

"It's okay." He sat at the couch and opened his laptop on the coffee table. Donovan had claimed the film had actual dialog, but he'd been sorely mistaken. All of Kris' acting would come without words.

"What's the first scene?"

"First?" Kris blurted. "There's only one. They'll shoot one camera angle at me sitting outside the window. The rest will be pointed at the pair in the bed. I watch, touch myself and get horny, then barge into the room. I end up behind the guy on top and turn him into the meat in the middle of the sandwich. At the end, I get to remark that it was fun meeting the new neighbors and then exit. Want to help with that line?"

"Sure. Hit me." Zayn widened his stance. "Ready."

He glanced down at the three lines, then back up at Zayn. Kris imagined his two co-stars in Zayn's place. He groaned like he would right after sex. "Welcome to the neighborhood. It's a pleasure getting to meet the new renters."

He sounded corny, despite trying not to.

"That was horrible," Zayn said.

"I know." Kris massaged his temples. "I need to do it again."

"No, I meant the lines are horrible. Your delivery isn't great, but you've got crap to work with." Zayn perched on the arm of the couch. "You don't have the same enthusiasm like when you read for me at the studio."

"It's not exciting." Kris met Zayn's gaze. "Some licking, touching, blow jobs, then sex. Shouting, groaning and jizz everywhere. Boring."

"Don't you need to look like you're at least enjoying yourself?" Zayn asked. "You want people to buy into what you're selling, so to speak."

Zayn had a point. Kris laced his fingers together. He had to make Zayn see his side of the argument. "The last time you watched a dirty movie, did you watch it to see the performers acting like they liked what they were doing or because you wanted to get off?"

"Actually, the last porno I watched featured you and I'm not going to lie, I was horny. But, I liked what I saw because it was you in the movie."

Kris paused. He'd never expected Zayn to say that. Shit. "That's silly—I'm not that hot." He waggled his finger. "It was to check the titles on my résumé, wasn't it? I get it."

"You're really negative when someone tries to give you a compliment." Zayn plopped onto the couch beside him. "You said something about not being high on yourself. What did you mean?" He put one hand up. "If you don't want to say, that's fine. Just curious."

Kris debated his options. He'd never really told anyone about his past. Keeping everything locked inside had worked so much better. When he did let people in, either the person left him or smeared his name. Then again, the people he'd told were in the porn industry. Zayn wasn't, but he had the capability to screw Kris over. Fuck it. He needed to talk and Zayn seemed to want to listen.

"Do you remember high school?" Kris asked. Just asking the question brought back a wave of memories. His stomach ached. "It's been a while."

"A few years, yeah, but I do, faintly." Zayn tipped his head slightly and nodded once. "Go ahead."

"Remember how there are stereotypical kids? The jocks, dorks, geeks, the band kids, et cetera. I was the drama geek. No muscle tone, all legs and arms, and fully in love with the theater. I saw myself on the stages of New York. I'd work with the stars and find a handsome man to live with and get my happily ever after."

"Nothing wrong with that. Those are good dreams."

"I also had a crazy crush on the captain of the football team, but I never said anything." He sighed. "High school kids don't give a shit about the theater. I spent more time getting my ass kicked than I did working on my lines. I went off to college for a semester to get away from my problems. That three months with other thespians got me thinking I could make it not in New York but in Hollywood. Pretty much everyone said I wouldn't and I wanted to prove them wrong. Truth was, I wanted to get away from a bad situation."

He'd tell some of his truths, but not all. Not yet. He refused to leave everything on the table.

"Ex-boyfriend?" Zayn draped his arm across the back of the sofa. "Or hadn't you come out yet?"

"I'd come out. It was fashionable then." He scrubbed both hands over his face. "No, I had a guy who was supposed to be my boyfriend, who was my first official fuck, turn on me." He shivered. Even thinking about the past stirred up feelings he'd hoped were buried. The scars ripped open all over again. "He walked into rehearsal for whatever play we were putting on and told everyone my limp dick wasn't going to get me out of the state of Ohio. I was worthless as a boyfriend and actor. I never got a chance to show them I could perform."

"Why?"

"I left the building, the city and the state all in one day. I haven't looked back, except to think about what I might have done differently."

"He was a dick." Zayn rubbed Kris' back. "No, seriously. He never should've done that. Makes me think he had the small penis."

"He was hung like a horse." Kris stood and paced the length of the room. "Because of him, I decided I wasn't going to bottom for anyone ever again."

"You were treated like shit. It's understandable."

Zayn didn't have to be so understanding. He didn't. If he'd go back to being an ass, he'd give Kris the reasons to keep distance between them.

"Anyway, I got into porn because it was easy and profitable. Not my best move, but when you're hungry, you do things you're not proud of." Kris looked at the clock. Fuck. He needed to get going if he wanted to be on set on time. He rushed into the kitchen and filled Nugent's bowl. "Here you go, bud. I've got to make some money." He winced. He sounded so lame.

Nugent's tail thwacked against Kris' leg. He munched happily on his food.

"You've got demons, but you're not just a porn star. You're more." Zayn stuffed his hands into his pockets. "Trust me."

"I'm trying to." Kris waited for the dog to finish eating. "Ready to go outside? I'll stay out there with you." He followed Nugent onto the back patio.

"He really is a good dog." Zayn stood beside Kris. "Listens well and is behaved. You hit the jackpot."

"He's considered a dangerous breed, so I'll have to be extra careful, but I did." Kris smiled and opened the door for Nugent. "I couldn't have picked a better pet." Once everyone was inside, Kris locked the back door. "Do you want to ride with me, then?"

"I will." Zayn tossed his keys onto the table.

Kris picked up his bag, then patted Nugent. "I'll be back." He opened the front door. Zayn ducked under his arm and left the condo. Kris shook his head. Everything seemed way too easy. Zayn looked good in his home. They'd fallen into an easy banter and Zayn had managed to get him to open up about crap he hated to discuss. Then there was the attraction. He wanted to rip Zayn's clothes off and fuck him senseless. But the kiss... Zayn had pulled away. He locked the front door, then headed to the car.

"How far is the shoot?" Zayn eased onto the passenger seat. "Not far?"

"Half an hour away."

"Not bad." Zayn plunked his arm on the middle console. "So, tell me more about Donovan."

"He's an ass." Kris backed down the driveway. On the short street, he headed forward. Ten minutes later, he zipped along the freeway toward the shoot. "His main goal is money. Make as much money as possible on the backs of anyone he can con into working for him. He got into porn because it's easy. We fuck, he makes money."

"Ah. Gotcha." Zayn tapped the console. "Sounds like Myron."

"I don't know about that, but he's self-centered." Kris glanced over at Zayn. Even in Kris' car, Zayn relaxed more.

"He talks a lot and gets loud when he's wrong, doesn't he?"

"Yeah," Kris replied. He turned into the housing development where the shoot was taking place. "How'd you guess?"

"Just a hunch. He's the kind who screams when he's wrong, but never makes compliments. He loves to antagonize and will argue just for the sake of arguing," Zayn said. "Or is he arguing because he can't deal with ever being in the wrong?"

"Bingo." Kris parked in the expansive driveway. "This is it. The actual shoot is upstairs. The way the house is set up, it could be apartments."

"You've been here before?"

"Couple times." He winced again. "Sorry. I forget you're not in my business."

"Nothing to be ashamed of. You were doing your job." Zayn cracked his knuckles. "Speaking of doing a job, I'm about to do mine." He grinned and grabbed Kris' hand. "Promise. We'll get you out of this business and get you into a few mainstream movies."

Kris' heart leaped. He shouldn't get his hopes up, but damn. Zayn was persuasive. He tamped down the hope and headed into the mansion.

Donovan stood in the downstairs living room and paced. He shouted at his cell phone. "I don't care if he's got the plague. He said he'd be here. This doesn't work without him." When he caught sight of Kris, he swiped his fingers across the phone and smiled. "You're here. Good. Who is this?"

Zayn rushed past Kris. "Zayn Mason. I'm representing Kris Hunter. As of today, this is the last movie he'll be making in the adult genre."

"Really?" Donovan's dark eyebrows knotted. "Since when?" He adjusted his pants, hiking them up his hips. "You love making this stuff."

Kris hesitated. He kind of liked hearing someone stand up for him. He'd held his ground on his own for so long. The help relieved him.

"While the thrill of filming might still be here, Kris is planning on moving on." Zayn matched Donovan's stance. "We make this movie and that's it. No more contacting my client. Understood?"

"No." Donovan narrowed his eyes. "But since you said we, I'm assuming you're participating? We do need a third."

Fuck. This was what Kris had anticipated.

"Two things. One, I only fuck one person and he's Kris. Two, we never film our sessions," Zayn said. "So, either you get this going with him and the other man or you void the contract and we go our merry way."

"You can't do that," Donovan growled. "He's mine."

"Yours?" Kris snapped. Hell, he wasn't even sure when he'd signed on to have sex with Zayn. Not that he didn't want to sleep with his so-called agent, but still.

"Okay. We're obviously not on the same page. Let me simplify this." Zayn folded his hands and glared at Donovan. "After this movie, don't call my client. He's done. Understood? He doesn't belong to you and won't be working for you."

"That's bullshit." Donovan shook his head. "This is all bullshit. He's been my best performer. Fucking hell." His tone rose along with the volume. "I'm not giving up. No fucking way." Donovan stomped off, leaving Kris and Zayn alone.

"Well, that went well." Zayn turned to face Kris. "He's angry, but I got through to him."

"Oh yeah. Pissing him off is great." Kris groaned. "But you did do what I asked. I need to get changed. Just stay out of the way and you can watch. Hell, having a real voyeur might improve my performance." He shouldn't have said that, but after the sex comment, he didn't care.

"I can watch? Cool." Zayn grabbed the front of Kris' shirt. "I was too forward about what you and I are doing, but I said it to put him in his place."

"So I'm your bitch?" Kris brushed past Zayn. He needed to get ready and get away from Zayn for a bit. His brain swam. He hated to be teased and Zayn definitely teased him.

He ducked into the seclusion of the downstairs bathroom and changed clothes. His skin still prickled from Zayn's touch. He liked being around Zayn, but he wasn't sure what to think of the guy. One minute he seemed attracted to Kris, then the next he was behaving like they were nothing more than business partners. The shifts in mentality drove him berserk.

He stepped into the threadbare jeans, then his boots. He cringed. Wearing boots, or any shoes for that matter, without socks grossed him out. Still, the role called for him to go sans socks. He stared at himself in the mirror and tied the necktie around his throat. Was the thing supposed to be tight? Loose? Casual? He loosened the knot. Casual sounded much better.

Kris rubbed baby oil into his skin to make his body shimmer. Each rub and caress over his chest turned him on. His thoughts turned to Zayn. He'd have a voyeur. Yes, Zayn had watched him in the videos, but this would be live. Damn it, he was going to give his business partner a real view. He pinched his nipples, making them stand out. A peal of desire surged through him. He groaned. Hell yes. He wanted Zayn begging for him.

See what you're missing? Stop being a waffling douche and you can have me. He flexed his muscles, then nodded. Time to head out to the shoot.

Kris strode onto the set. He knew each of the camera men and the guys working the lights. The crew wasn't as big as on some of the films. He thanked God for that.

"Okay, Kris, go onto the balcony. As far as we're concerned for this film, that's the walkway up to the apartment. Gerry, I want you on the bed in here. You're already nude and playing with yourself. Get that dick nice and hard." Donovan pointed. "I want to film Kris through the window. Fix the lighting so we can see him."

Kris ducked through the open door to the balcony. He stood in the chill of the night air and watched the scene unfold in the bedroom. If people only knew how much work and how many details went into porn, they might appreciate it more. Or they'd be horrified.

Half an hour later, Donovan growled at the young man working the clapper board. The kid, old enough to be working on the set but looking way too young for the business, signaled the start of the scene.

One of the camera men pointed to Kris, letting him know it was time to do the walk up the balcony to the door. He made the fifteen-step journey, then stopped when he heard the groaning. He turned to the glass and peered at the person in the bed.

Just as the script claimed, he raked his fingers through his hair, then leaned against the wall. He propped one foot up on the rocks and slid both hands over his crotch. Instead of getting hard because of Gerry whacking off, he did because he knew Zayn was in the shadows, watching. He caught Zayn's glance.

Like what you see? Kris massaged the bulge in his pants. *Want my cock? I want to feel my dick so far up your ass you won't be able to tell where you end and I begin.*

Zayn's lips parted. He'd folded his arms and leaned against the doorframe. When Kris popped the button on his own jeans and slipped one hand into the denim, Zayn's eyes widened.

"Oh God," Gerry moaned. "I need fucked so bad. So bad."

Kris froze. *Shit.* That was the cue for him to stop masturbating himself and to go into the bedroom. He eased his hand from behind his pants, then opened the door to Gerry's room. Although he should be paying attention to the man on the bed, he positioned himself so he could steal glances at Zayn. He stepped out of his jeans, then removed the necktie.

With each touch and caress, his desire heightened. Now if he could've had someone like Zayn in the background, he might have been able to put more enthusiasm into his performances. His cock throbbed. He longed to rub himself, then stalk across the room and drag the clothes off Zayn.

"Holy fucking hell." Gerry yanked Kris' hair. "I'm...coming."

Kris pulled away from Gerry long enough to tilt his on-screen lover's cock toward Gerry's belly. Gerry shivered. He spurted all over his abs.

"Damn," he said, drawing the word out. He sagged against the bed. "I didn't know you could do that."

Kris wiped his mouth, then stood. "I didn't think I'd have such a hot neighbor." He grabbed a condom from the box, then sheathed himself. "I'm going to fuck that neighbor." He shoved Gerry's knees toward his chest, folding him in half. When he glanced over to where Zayn stood, he noticed his friend wasn't there. *What the hell? Shit.*

"Yeah. Fuck me." Gerry tugged his ass cheeks, opening his hole. "I need a good reaming."

Kris focused on the rest of what he had to do for the film and getting off. Screw it. If Zayn didn't want to watch any longer, then fine. He had a job he had to do. Kris dribbled lube over Gerry's hole, then his own cock. He lined his dick up, then pushed into Gerry's body. Before long he built up a good speed. The headboard knocked against the wall and the springs on the bed creaked.

Kris grabbed Gerry's ankles and pistoned his hips. In and out. He slammed his balls against Gerry's ass. Although he wasn't terribly turned on any longer, he needed to come. The film wouldn't finish if he didn't splatter his seed all over Gerry.

He focused on the hunger he'd seen in Zayn's eyes. He wanted to bring back that desire and kick it up a few notches. The heat in his body spiraled out to his limbs. Yes, imprinting another face over Gerry's, even if only in his mind, wasn't cool, but Kris would get off. A growl bubbled in Kris' throat. He pushed deep into Gerry.

"Fucking balls." Every fiber of Kris' being screamed to stay in Gerry when he came. Instead Kris pulled out. He yanked the rubber off his cock, then stroked himself until his seed streaked across Gerry's stomach.

"Damn. Hell yeah." Gerry lowered his legs. He panted on the bed and stared at Kris. "Best fuck of my life."

"Better be." Kris bent long enough to pick his pants and tie off the floor, then grabbed his boots. "Welcome to the neighborhood."

"Come back any time." Gerry waved, albeit weakly. "I'm ready when you're willing."

"Uh-huh." Kris donned his pants, then strode out of the bedroom.

"Cut," Donovan shouted. "Great. Take it to editing." He clapped his hands. "Wow. I'm stunned."

Kris wandered back into the bedroom. "Why?"

"You were great. I've never seen you come alive like that." Donovan draped his arm around Kris' shoulders. "How much? I'll pay whatever you ask if you'll come back and do that again."

"I'm done." Kris held out his hand. "I want my check. Double the normal amount."

"You're a shit." Donovan snapped his fingers. "Where is my assistant?"

The young man who'd used the clapperboard hurried up to Donovan's side. "Here."

"Go. Start picking up the gear." Donovan handed over the check. "Where is your agent?"

"I'm right here." Zayn strolled into the bedroom. "I've seen everything. We're done here, correct?"

"I—I don't want him to go." Donovan grabbed for Kris. "He's my best performer. You can't let him leave the business." He clapped on to Zayn's arm. "What is your angle? You're fucking him? Feeding him drugs? Alcohol? Mind-fucks? What?"

"I'm treating him with dignity…something you've probably never heard of." Zayn slid his hand into Kris'. "Come on. We're out of here." He tugged Kris through the house to the first floor, then out to the driveway. "Much better."

"What? Slow down. Where is my bag?" Kris dug in his heels. "I need my stuff."

"I got it already." Zayn held up the keys. "I couldn't stay in there any longer." He pointed to the bag in the backseat. "I grabbed it while you were performing."

"Ah." Kris didn't move. "I need a shower and food. Are you planning on driving? Or what?"

"Tell me where to turn and I'll drive so you can rest." When Kris still didn't move, Zayn added, "Go through the bag. I can tell you don't trust me. Everything is there and here's your check."

He didn't have anything worthy of being stolen. Hell, his clothes and wallet weren't that exciting. He didn't carry any credit cards and kept a small amount of money on his person. Something else bothered him.

"Why did you leave?" Kris asked. He folded the check and tucked it into his back pocket. "I don't understand."

"Let's get in the car. I don't want prying ears to hear." Zayn waved Kris over to the vehicle. "Yeah?"

"Fine." Kris flopped onto the passenger seat. He was being a shit and had no right to get upset with Zayn. But come on. He'd left! He'd been Kris' motivation on the film.

"Let's get on the road." Zayn backed down the driveway, then pulled out onto the road. "Okay. Why did I leave, right?"

"Yeah. We had something going. I got off because you were there," Kris snapped. "I actually looked like I was having fun. Donovan even believed me."

"I know." Zayn merged into traffic. "I noticed. Your spark came back and I saw glimpses of the actor that showed up at the audition yesterday."

"And that was so bad that you had to leave?"

"It wasn't bad. Far from it." Zayn gripped the steering wheel. "I saw the real man and understood why all the porn directors want you. It has nothing to do with your cock—which is very nice."

"Then?" His voice cracked. He hadn't meant to sound so needy, but his ego had taken a beating when Zayn walked out.

"You turned me on," Zayn whispered. "Watching you with him made me want to jump in the middle, but I can't."

"Why?" Kris turned his full attention to Zayn. "What happened?"

Zayn pointed. "Is this the turn?"

"Yeah, make a right here and we'll end up at my neighborhood." Kris sighed. "Never mind. It's not my business."

"Hold up." Zayn maneuvered down the winding roads to Kris' condo. "It is your business. This one?"

"That's my condo, yeah. Isn't that your Jag in the driveway?"

"Sorry." He parked beside the Jaguar, then turned off the car. "Can we go inside and talk?"

"Sure. I need to take care of Nugent first, but we can." Kris left the vehicle, then grabbed his bag from the back seat. He unlocked the front door. Nugent surged to his side and licked his hand. "Hey, bud. Didja miss me?"

Nugent barked twice, then danced around Kris' feet. At least the dog was happy to see him. He wasn't so sure about Zayn. He switched on the patio light, then opened the back door. "Come on, Nuge." When the dog went outside, Kris followed. He wished he still smoked. Then he'd have something for his hands to do.

Zayn didn't join him, making Kris' spirits sink even more.

The dog pottied, then went inside. Kris followed him. He found Zayn on the couch with his elbows on his knees.

"Okay. I'll bite. What's wrong?" Kris pulled a T-shirt from the laundry basket, then sat on the coffee table. "You're not the first person to ever walk out on me. It's not a big deal. Really. I'll live."

"It's not that." Zayn shoved his hair off his forehead and met Kris' gaze. "I left because I was turned on. I wanted to be with you and I can't. Putting my heart out on the line is something I'm not ready to do, but every time I look at you...you're dangerous to me."

Kris bit back his shock. He hadn't expected Zayn to actually be attracted to him. Yes, there was the awkward kiss, but it was just that—awkward. The porn star side of him could try to con Zayn into his bed. The desire bubbled between them enough for a hot time in the sack. But the side of him that wanted to be a proper actor held him in check. If he was going to reach his goal, he had to do it without sex.

"Then we make a pact. You help me with my acting so I can get into mainstream films and I won't act on our mutual desire. Sound like a deal?" Kris asked.

"Deal." Zayn nodded. "Good deal."

Kris sighed. He wanted to make good on the promise, but he knew better. He'd fallen into lust with Zayn Mason and nothing short of them fucking each other senseless was going to get the casting director out of his system.

Chapter Five

Zayn's heart sank. This *wasn't* how he wanted things to go. Yes, he wanted Kris to work with him. Yes, he wanted them to become friends. But there was the attraction. He'd been a fool to push Kris away. Hell, he'd fallen in lust the first time he'd seen him, but pushed those feelings aside. He wasn't going to get involved with anyone. Except the more time he spent with Kris, the more he liked him.

"I need to go." Zayn stood. He pulled his phone from his pocket. The little icons at the top of the screen flashed. Probably his email overflowing. He shook his head. He shouldn't have ignored his other duties for so long, but he believed in Kris.

"Sure." Kris stood and crossed the room to the front door. "It's been pretty intense today. Thanks, I appreciate the help."

"It's not you." Zayn pressed his lips together. Damn it. He'd screw this up if he kept talking.

"I get it—whatever it is. We can't be fuck friends if we're going to work together. Makes sense." Kris smiled, but the magic wasn't there.

"Just...shit." Zayn scrubbed both hands over his face, despite holding his phone. "I've got your email on your résumé, right?"

Kris nodded.

"Okay. I'll email the horror script to you when I get home. Read it over and call me—I'll include my personal number. If you think it's something you want to do, I'll get in touch with the director and get the audition set up." Zayn hesitated. The scent of Kris' cologne along with sweat curled around him. He'd always been a sucker for a sweaty, hardworking guy. His common sense screamed to leave, but his heart yearned for Kris. Zayn leaned forward and kissed him.

God, he wanted this connection. He pressed his body to Kris' and moaned. When he bit Kris' bottom lip, Kris groaned. Kris smoothed his hands along Zayn's chest. The tingles shot straight along his skin to his groin. Why was he walking away?

Kris eased his arms between him and Zayn. "Sorry." He didn't look at Zayn. "I should let you go."

Right now wasn't the right time to explain all the things running through his head. Zayn nodded. "Okay. Talk to you tomorrow?"

"Sure." Kris backed away from Zayn and shut the screen door. He didn't glance out the window or hover by the door. Instead, he disappeared into the condo.

Zayn went to his car, then slid behind the wheel. He drove across town to his own apartment. He couldn't get Kris out of his head. He kept seeing moments from the porn movie when he closed his eyes. The man was electric. Sure, he was naked and fucking someone else, but while Zayn had watched the scene unfold, he didn't feel like he was watching a scene. He *believed* the desire between the two men.

He parked in his designated spot, then left the car and closed the garage door. He knew damn well Kris wasn't in love or even in lust with his costar. From the moment the filming had started, Zayn had noticed the crackle wasn't there. But when Kris had caught Zayn's glance, he'd come alive. The movie had taken flight.

Zayn trudged up the steps to his floor, then made his way into his apartment. Once inside, he dropped his tablet and phone onto the table, then went into his bedroom. He'd pulled more than a few all-nighters and even those didn't bring out the bone-deep weariness he felt. He flopped on the bed.

He stared into the blackness of his room and stuffed both hands into his pants. "I'm sorry," he said aloud. "I don't trust easily. I don't like to rely on others. I'm crap in a relationship and even worse in bed, but I'm attracted to you." The vision of Kris in the nude formed in his mind. "I want you. I can't have you, but I can't get you out of my brain."

He shoved his pants down his hips, then wrapped both hands around his cock. He squeezed his eyes closed and stroked himself. In his mind, he took over the role of Kris' costar. He wanted the hunky neighbor to break into his apartment and fuck him until he screamed. He replayed the movie in his brain, but from his own vantage point. He met Kris' gaze.

"Please. I need you to fuck me." Zayn reached for Kris. Although Kris wasn't there, Zayn imagined Kris breaching his hole. The burn resonated to his core. He stroked harder and faster on his cock. "Jesus. Please."

Kris didn't reply. Instead, he slammed into Zayn. His lips parted and a fine sheen of sweat glistened on his forehead and chest. He gritted his teeth.

Zayn groaned. *Oh hell.* He wasn't going to hold back the orgasm. From his toes to his hairline, he tensed. His balls vibrated and his cock twitched. Cum shot onto his belly and the bottom half of his shirt. He blew out a long breath.

"Shit," he muttered. He opened his eyes. Fantasizing about Kris wasn't going to get Kris a job. Hell, it wasn't even going to help Zayn fall asleep that night.

He cleaned the jizz off his stomach, then removed his shirt. He shucked his jeans and underwear. After a shower, he stepped into a pair of sleep pants. Time to help Kris and get his head into the game.

Zayn opened his laptop. He logged into his email, then located Kris' email address. Once he found the script and the contact information for the horror movie, he forward the info to Kris. He included his phone number too.

"Call me. Please?" Zayn whispered. He scanned his other emails. Three were job offers to work on other motion pictures. Two of the movies were lower-budget flicks being made by friends and the other involved Myron again. Great. Myron wanted to work with him even more?

Zayn replied to the various emails. He wanted to work on the smaller films. Truth be told, he wanted Kris in at least one of them.

He sat back in his seat and folded his hands behind his head. "I got you out of that business. Now trust me to get you going in my world."

* * * *

The next morning, Zayn called his contacts on all three movies. He accepted a job with the largest film in order to cast the handful of characters. He also agreed to work on the smaller pictures.

"Tom, I've already got some ideas for this movie." Zayn tapped his stylus on the edge of his tablet. Once he'd read the script for the romantic comedy, he'd immediately seen the characters in his mind. All he needed to do was convince the right actors to accept the respective parts.

"Who?" Tom asked. "I'm on a tight deadline."

"I've got a shortlist for the character of Kate and have emailed those I think would fit. I'm holding the casting call this weekend. As for Ronald, I think I know who you want." Zayn wrote Kris' name under Ronald's name.

"As long as you get the job done, I'm happy." Tom hung up, leaving Zayn alone with his thoughts.

Zayn dialed Kris' number. They needed to talk and not just about the various roles. The line rang three times before Kris answered.

"Hi," Kris said. "May I ask who is calling?"

So proper and mannered. Sexy. "It's Zayn. I've got some leads for you and need to talk with you about them. Do you have time?"

"I do."

Not a long answer, but it would work. "Did you get my email? I sent two scripts."

"I did. I've read them both and prepped. When are the auditions?" Kris asked.

"You're ready?" Zayn rubbed his forehead. Maybe that was part of the problem—Kris didn't prep enough. Then again, some actors worked fast. Once they were on set, they had to learn lines fast. Maybe he'd better give Kris a shot. "Read me the lead from *Crusher*. Read Joe's part. First scene. Convince me you're Joe."

"You don't know there's a ghost out there, Rina. It's a legend. No one has ever shot video of him. Ignore the stories and let's go. It's our last weekend before I leave."

Zayn nodded once. *Not bad.* He found Rina's line. "It's scary out there. I don't want the ghost to get me." God. This was crap for the female lead. She deserved better lines.

"You'll be with me. No ghost is going to get you," Kris murmured. "I won't let them."

Again, not the greatest writing, but the soft tone of Kris' voice helped convince Zayn. Hell, he'd go into the woods with Kris. "You've convinced me."

"We'll have a good weekend. One to remember. One for those nights while you're at college and feeling low. You know, when you want to play with that sweet pussy. Think of me and what we did this weekend." Kris didn't laugh. Most actors would've cracked a chuckle because of the word pussy. Then again, if Zayn had been writing the lines, he would've chucked that one after the first draft.

"Good." Zayn scribbled some notes onto his tablet on the notepad function. "I'd try to dress for the part too. I'll call Paul and get back to you. Sound good?"

"Thanks."

Zayn hesitated. He didn't want to let Kris go. "Wait."

"I'm here." No inflection in his voice.

"I like spending time with you." He held his breath. Opening himself up wasn't his strong point. He got others to bare their souls, not him.

"Thanks."

Shit. He wanted more. "Do you like coffee?"

"I do."

At least he still had Kris talking. "What if I bring some over? I'll work with you and instead of the calling back and forth, you'll get real-time information. Sound like a plan?" *I need to see you.*

"Okay. I'll look for you."

He hadn't turned Zayn down. Thank God. "I'll be there in forty-five. See you." Zayn swiped his finger over the screen to end the call. He needed a plan beyond bringing coffee. He dialed Paul's number and waited two rings. "Paul? It's Zayn."

"Got a leading man for me?" Paul asked.

"I do. When do you want to see him?"

"Five. I've got the female lead coming in. Will that work for you? Studio C at Technical City."

"Perfect. I'll get him there." Zayn blew out a long breath. Okay. Grab coffee on the way to Kris'. Simple. Get Kris to the studio. Easy. Convince Kris this pairing wasn't a bad idea...talk about the impossible. He tucked his phone, tablet and wallet into his messenger bag. Passion should never be extinguished.

Zayn sped across town to Kris' condo. Odd, but he felt like he was going home. He'd lived at his apartment for nearly five years, but the place never quite felt like permanence. Something else would come along to make him move or change...

He zipped down the highway, then turned onto the exit for Kris' development. For the last three years, he'd convinced himself he wasn't going to get involved with anyone. How could he change his mind after one night together? Because he'd seen one of the most intimate acts performed by Kris. If that's what they guy did for a porn shoot, then God help Zayn, he wanted to see Kris in the bedroom without the cameras.

He stopped at his favorite drive-through coffee house and picked up two tall cups of java. Before he left, he made sure to request plenty of additives. Riding with coffees in a Jaguar wasn't smart, but he'd be careful. He needed to get to Kris.

He drove down the short street to Kris' place. When he parked, he noticed a guy standing on the lawn next door. The man glared at Zayn.

Zayn rolled his eyes. Some people were jerks. He grabbed his bag and the box with the cups, then locked the car.

"Are you dating Kris?" the guy called.

"Your point?" Zayn bit back a smile. He liked his noncommittal answer.

"You know he's queer, right?"

"You asked if I was dating him, so I'd assume I'd know he was gay. Is that a problem for you?" Zayn strode up the walkway, then stopped at the front door. "It's not a problem for me."

"You're sick," the neighbor spat.

"Oh well." Zayn knocked on Kris' door. The dog barked on the other side of the wall. After a moment, Kris appeared in the doorway. "Hi." Zayn held up the coffee. "I grabbed black, but with sugar, cream and pretty much anything else you can put in a cup."

"Thanks." Kris stood out of the way while Zayn entered the condo. "Did Henry say something? He's being a dick."

"He did, but it's cool. I don't mind."

"Ever since I took Nugent, Henry's been strange. It's like he's expecting me to do something dumb or treat the dog like shit. I don't know."

"He wants to cause trouble. I'd ignore him." Zayn placed his bag on the couch, then offered over the coffees. "So, I got you the audition for five tonight. It's at Technical Artists, Studio C. You'll read for Joe. Cool?"

"Thanks." Kris almost grinned. The curl of his lips formed, but he didn't quite smile. "I'll be ready."

"I know you will. You nailed it when you called me." Zayn sat opposite Kris at the table. "Can I level with you?"

"Sure." Kris shrugged. "It's a free country." Not the nicest reception, but not totally icy either.

Zayn wasn't sure where to begin. So many words teetered on the tip of his tongue, but he feared speaking. If he allowed himself to be raw, he risked his heart and soul. He didn't want rejection again, but he also didn't want to haul his baggage around.

"I'm not a very open person," Zayn said finally.

"I couldn't tell." Kris sipped the coffee, then dumped two packets of cream and a packet of sugar into the brew. "I thought it was just you being professional."

"I'm trying to keep my work life and my personal life separate, but there are times when it's lonely." Zayn wrapped his hands around his cup. If he didn't start talking, he'd never let go of the past. "I'm thirty-two years old and have had four serious boyfriends in my life. Guys either see me as a stepping stone to the big time or they want to walk all over me because they can't imagine sticking around with the help for all that long." He traced the design of the cup with the tip of his thumb. "I keep myself closed off because it's easier than getting hurt. I've kept the sides of my life separate because I've had them clash and it sucks."

"You don't have to explain." Kris shrugged again. "We haven't gone on a date. A couple of kisses don't amount to much. I'm not upset. Now I know the boundaries and I'm okay with it."

"You might not be upset, but I am." He gripped the cup tighter. So many thoughts bombarded him. He drew in a long breath then let it out. "I've wanted to talk about this crap for a long time."

"I'm listening." This time Kris did smile. "Whatever it is, I'm here." Not pandering, but an honest, open concern shone on Kris' face. His eyes twinkled. Zayn wondered if he'd be just as sexy and sweet first thing in the morning.

"You look like you're a million miles away again." Kris waved his hand in front of Zayn's face. "What are you thinking? Can't be about my fantastic acting or getting me a role."

"I'm thinking I want to see that drive come out in everything you do. You're a good man."

"I try. Doesn't always work."

The tips of Kris' ears burned red and he averted his gaze. Zayn tipped his head to the side. Had he touched a nerve? He'd have to make things up to Kris later.

"That's what I like about you—among other things. You're sincere. If you say you're listening, I believe you. I haven't always had that." He stared at the ripples in his coffee. He'd said too much by admitting one of his truths, but who cared? If they could be honest with each other, he'd not only feel better about the crap in his past, but maybe he'd motivate Kris' performances in the auditions. "My first real boyfriend was when I was just out of high school. We parted on good terms, but he also introduced me to my next boyfriend, Jaden. God. I was so hung up on him, but he was bisexual. The jerk had me strung along thinking we were going to last. We weren't. He wanted threesomes, but never bothered to tell me. He dicked me over."

"I understand. I had a boyfriend who wanted to be in the porn. I thought he was still building his cred. No, he'd already done some. Sucked. He became bigger than me—not that I care. I'd rather not be big in this business." Kris chuckled. "You've probably heard of him. Jonah Boner. Stupid name, but he loves it.

Anyhow, the big dick was really trying to conquer every new man in porn. He had a list or something. I was a notch on his bedpost, so to speak."

"I've heard of him, but not that mentality. Although, the method doesn't surprise me. That's why a lot of leading men jump from woman to woman to woman. They want to say they've done most of Hollywood." He grabbed Kris' hand. "Since we're name-dropping, have you ever heard of Ascher Flohr? He was up for a few awards last season. Did a couple of dramas that required him to cry on cue." When Kris nodded, Zayn continued. "Because of him, my third boyfriend left me. Bobby wanted to be his bitch. Completely unabashedly wanted to be owned by Ascher. From what I've gleaned in the gossip rags, it worked for a while. I don't know what he's up to right now — Ascher *or* Bobby."

Kris squeezed Zayn's fingers. "You got to move forward, right?" He glanced around the room. "I don't know. The way we keep bringing up exes, I feel like we should be doing shots or something. Mention an ex and do a shot."

"We'd be wasted in no time."

"Probably. It's a little early for booze too."

"Some days it's not, but I hear you." Zayn met Kris' smile. He liked being able to grin with someone. But he needed to finish. He held Kris' hand. "I did way too many shots when Bobby left me. I thought I was drowning my sorrow. I wasn't and I couldn't move forward. Enter Eli."

Kris bopped his head back and forth. "I hear a dum, dum, dum when you say his name. It was bad, wasn't it?"

"You have no idea. He's the reason I'm not in the dating pool. The dickhead. We were together for three years. Three fucking years. I loved him." The memories stung. He winced and stared at his hand on his lap. "I really loved him and wish he would've been honest with me."

"What'd he do?"

Zayn sighed. Once he started to explain Eli, he wouldn't be able to stop. But he needed to talk. "He wanted to be in the movies. The whole time we were together, he secretly wanted me to put him in a motion picture. He never actually told me so and expected me to figure it out by osmosis, I guess." He snorted. "I should've seen it coming after some of the things he'd said and did. When he went with me to award shows, he always jumped in front of the cameras. If someone interviewed me, he was right there. I thought he was just excited. Turned out he was trying to get face time. He wanted someone to discover him and since I hadn't put him in a big budget movie, he moved on. Resentment set in because I wasn't helping him. That resentment turned to sheer hate. I didn't know he hated me. I thought it was just a phase. By the time we decided to call it quits, he already had another boyfriend who was a director. I never found out who the guy was, but I've heard they were happy."

He wobbled on his chair. He'd been wrung out from head to his toe. The tension in his arms flowed out of him and he sighed. Although others in his circle of friends had witnessed the implosion with Eli, Zayn had never told anyone else about his problems. Being able to talk freed him and Kris had been a good listener. The boulder he'd carried around seemed to roll away when he was with Kris. The depression was still ingrained in him, but not as deep. He glanced over at Kris again.

"Sorry. I shouldn't have unloaded all that on you." He looked into Kris' eyes, then tore his gaze away. "It's been a long time. Eli has been a wound that wouldn't heal." But after talking, the pain lessened. He kissed Kris' knuckles. An intimate gesture, but oh so right.

Kris didn't frown or pull away. "Corny as this sounds, everyone needs a chance to talk." He toyed with the lip of his cup with his free hand. "I know I need to sometimes. I bottle lots of things up."

Zayn understood far too well. "It's just hard when you can't trust someone. Here's me, not wanting to date because I'm convinced my life will go to pot if I do. Then I pull the same shit I don't want happening to me, on you. It's not fair and I'm sorry." Again, he shouldn't have dumped so much on his friend, but the more he said, the better he felt.

"Don't worry about it." Kris grinned. "Stuff happens. Wires get crossed. I get it."

"I *will* worry about what happened. Those two kisses weren't nothing. Double negative aside, I liked kissing you. For the first time in a long while, I felt alive. The initial kiss caught me off guard, but the second one...I thought about it all last night. I replayed the memories of your movie over and over. Wished I was in that guy's position, being fucked by you."

"You did?" Kris stared at Zayn. His eyes widened. "I didn't think it affected you."

"Oh yeah. You did." Zayn's cheeks heated. Tingles started in his belly and headed south of his belt. His cock throbbed. He wanted to shuck his clothes so they could explore their feelings for each other.

"We can't do this. Not now." Kris reached for Zayn, holding both hands. "I've got the audition in a couple hours."

"Let's plan on celebrating when you get the part." Zayn grinned. He stood and leaned across the table. Maybe he shouldn't try the kiss again, but the moment seemed so right. He wrapped his fingers around the back of Kris' neck and nipped Kris' bottom lip.

"You said I was dangerous." Kris' hot breath feathered over Zayn's cheeks. "I don't know about that, but I do know I want to nail this part so we can do that celebrating."

"Then let's practice. I want you to win the director over too." Zayn settled in his chair. He shouldn't be so attracted to Kris. Shouldn't want more of his kisses, but he did. "Did you look at the other script? It's a rom-com, but it's a good fit for you."

"I haven't." Kris tapped the keys on his laptop. "*Foxy*?"

"Yes." He switched into professional mode. Although he wanted Kris to pin him to the wall and kiss him senseless, they needed to prep for the role. "The premise is a mom who is tired of being such. She wants out of her rut. Really, she wants her old man to pay attention to her. She ends up kind of having an affair with her son's hockey coach. I'm thinking you'd be great in the husband role."

"I'd have to kiss a girl." Kris laughed. "Haven't done that in a while."

"You can do it."

"I hope so." Kris switched the laptop from standard mode to tablet mode. "Okay, so the guy is roughly thirty years old, married to his high school sweetheart and immersed in his job as a school teacher. Wow, haven't been one of those who keeps his clothes on." Kris laughed again. "I won't know what to do with myself."

"You'll manage. So, how would you prepare for the role? What's this guy thinking?" Zayn asked. "Get into his head."

"Well, he's a teacher, so he's smart. He's immersed in his job and from what I can tell, he takes it too seriously. I'd say he's one of those people who can't do something half-assed, unless he doesn't know he's doing it that way. I'd read the books in the subject he teaches and work on my poise. Teachers are held to a higher standard, so I'd have to look professional."

"Good. Read scene three. He doesn't have many lines, but it's important." Zayn pointed to the tablet. "Page seventy, I think."

Kris swiped through the pages. "Found it." He cleared his throat, then exhaled. "You're going to be the wife, right?"

"Oh, yeah." Zayn moved his chair from across the table to beside Kris. He located the right line. "Have you ever been bored? You know, with stuff?"

"I'm never bored. I've got too much to do. Papers to grade, lessons to plan. I've got to figure out how to get the budget to stretch so I can get those magazines for my sixth period class." Kris thrust his fingers into his hair. "Speaking of sixth period, I need to add notes on the battle of Gettysburg to the lesson."

"I see. You have no idea." Zayn watched Kris as he delivered the lines.

"I've been bored. You should see me during that blasted study hall. I've got other things I could be doing, but no. I'm babysitting. I can't get anything done because the moment you stop watching the students, they pull stunts. It's horrible." Kris spoke with gusto. He gestured along with the words and seemed to be enmeshed in the character.

"Yeah, that study hall from hell." Zayn rolled his eyes. "I would hate to be you."

"Are you being sarcastic?" Kris draped his arm around Zayn's shoulders. "Come on. What are you bored with? You've got two great kids, a house full of stuff to do and a husband who loves you. You're pretty lucky."

"I don't feel lucky."

"I don't understand." He turned to face Zayn. "You love the kids."

"I do, but I don't want my life to revolve around them. What am I going to do when the kids leave?" Zayn asked.

"Go back to school. Finish your degree in art. Why don't you look into some classes? I haven't seen you paint in a long time."

"I hate to paint."

Kris laughed. "You're such a kidder. You love painting." He laughed again and shook his head. "You know how to make me feel better. I've been wracking my brain, trying to figure out how to add that battle information to the lesson, and you've helped me. I know what I want to do. Thanks, babe." Kris kissed Zayn's temple, then left the table. He walked down the hallway a bit and then stopped. "So?"

Zayn considered his answer. If he were the one casting the film, Kris was a definite candidate. A top two, really. But he wasn't choosing. "You're golden. Give that delivery. I believed you were the teacher and kind of got a little pissed with you for not listening."

"Cool. When do I meet up for that audition?" Kris' eyes gleamed. "I want to go out for it."

"I'll call him in a few." Zayn checked his watch. "Strike that. I'll make the call while you're auditioning for the horror film."

"Cool," Kris said. "I'm going to get dressed for the part." He ducked into the bedroom, leaving Zayn alone.

Zayn folded his hands. Hell, he wasn't going to have to do much to sell Kris. The man sold himself with his work. Once he got his foot in the door with one film, he'd be unstoppable.

He switched the screens on his phone to the keypad and dialed the other director. Instead of getting through, he ended up talking to his friend's voice mail. Zayn stood and paced the length of the room. Seemed he liked to pace...or Kris just had him that much on edge. He massaged his temple and waited for the voicemail greeting to end so he could record his message.

"It's Zayn Mason. I've got the answer to your hero issue. Think you're going to like him. Call me back and I'll schedule a time for him to audition. You've got my number. Later." He hung up and slid the phone into his pants pocket.

"I'm ready." Kris strode into the living room. "What do you think? Casual, but cool and young."

Zayn drank in Kris' image. He'd worn another tight T-shirt. The cotton hugged his muscles in all the right places. His worn jeans featured just enough fraying to be stylish, but not trashy. The man knew how to work his clothes.

"Well?" Kris turned around, giving Zayn a better view. "Add the leather jacket? No?"

"I'd...I'm not sure if the movie is being filmed at night. He might have you wear a simple windbreaker instead. I'd go without. You're not expected to have the visual right at this point." Zayn crossed the room and splayed his hand on Kris' chest. "I like it."

"Yeah?" Kris asked. "I'm trying to make a good impression."

"You are." Zayn bit back a groan. Damn, the man made the right impression. He brought out all the dirty thoughts Zayn had hidden away. "You make me want to rip those clothes off you and lick every inch."

"You sound like one of my porn movies," Kris said. He bumped noses with Zayn as he lowered his head. "But better. I might have to have you put those thoughts into actions."

Zayn chuckled. He wasn't sure where he stood with Kris. Hell, he knew *what* he wanted to happen, but arguing with fate wasn't smart. Maybe a hot weekend would be good for them. Get the sexual tension dealt with, then move on to channel the passion to where it belonged—Kris' acting. Too bad Zayn already felt an attachment to Kris. In his soul, he knew they weren't going to just be friends or lovers short term. They were destined to be more. Now he had to hope his heart would survive the inevitable fall.

Chapter Six

Kris sat outside the audition room and rested his elbows on his knees. He'd done the best he could with the reading, but once the director found out what he did for his previous job...would he still be considered? He knew damn well he was a wild card. He could work out really well or be completely wrong for the part. If the director decided to focus on Kris' past, not his actual talent, he'd be sunk.

He scrubbed both hands over his face and groaned. He needed to think more positively, but he'd been down this road. Every time he got his hopes up and believed he could be really going mainstream, his hopes were dashed.

"Hey." Zayn bounded up to Kris. "You look like your dog died. He's okay, right?"

"Far as I know."

"Then what? They haven't made a decision yet." Zayn sat beside him and patted Kris' knee. "You'll be fine."

"As long as one of us thinks that. I've never had to wait right outside while the panel decided." Kris stood and strode over to the bank of windows overlooking a small courtyard. "Do you always make them wait?"

"No. I usually send them home and take the night to mull over the choices. Of course, with Rock, you were the easy choice, but that's me."

Kris stared at the trees swaying in the breeze. Orange light from the setting sun streaked across the space. He had to get his head out of the negative thoughts. "What about you? Have you heard anything?"

"I have." Zayn sat on the ledge and faced Kris. "I got a couple of calls for the both of us. Two concern other parts for you. I sent your demo reel to my friend with the romantic drama. He wants you. Even moved filming to the beginning of next month in order to start after the horror flick is done. If he couldn't have you, then he'd wait. Pretty cool, eh? I've got another audition lined up for another drama. It's a very small part, but it's a bigger picture. You'd be a cowboy. Think you could squeeze that into your schedule in two months?"

Kris blinked. *Wow.* "You're really working hard for me. I don't get it. You have no vested interest in me. I'm thrilled that you're helping, but I'm not sure what's in it for you." Kris folded his arms. The trees stopped moving. "Tell me?"

"I don't have a vested interest, other than wanting to see you succeed. You want to succeed, but you can't allow yourself to have hope." Zayn left his seat and stood beside Kris. "I get it. If you keep everything tamped down and held in, you can't be hurt. Getting out of porn means you're going to have to put yourself out there. You'll fall down, but you have to get back up."

"You sound like a greeting card. An atta' boy card or something." Kris faced Zayn. "But I like it. It's nice to have someone in my corner."

"Then it's a good thing I want to be in your corner. I like you, Kris." Zayn grasped Kris' hand. "I see the drive in you and know it should be channeled into something better than fucking someone on screen. If I haven't said that enough, then I should've because that's what I believe. You're good. You'll have to do some crowd scenes, but it's better than nothing."

Ah. He liked him as an actor. "Did you mean what you said about a victory celebration and fuck?" Kris laced his fingers with Zayn's. "You said you liked me, but in what way?"

"Kris." Zayn's gaze shifted to the side. "I can't — we — sorry. You've got company."

"It's because I did porn, isn't it? You don't want to be with me. I'm clean. I don't perform without knowing I'm clean and so are my costars." Kris pulled away from Zayn. "You could've said something earlier. The lies about the kiss, the crap about helping me."

"For fuck's sake, the director is here," Zayn growled.

The blood drained from Kris' face and his cheeks burned. He closed his eyes. He'd jumped to a conclusion and played the fool. God damn it.

"If you two are done having a lover's spat, I'd like to have a word with you, Kris," Paul said. "I've decided to cast you in the movie. We'll start filming next week. I hear you're good with tight deadlines and are fast at memorization. Name your agent — if he's not Zayn — and I'll email him the contracts." He stuck out his hand. "Congratulations."

"Thank you," Kris said. His heart lodged in his throat. *Holy crap. A contract. Wow.* "I'm thrilled. I won't let you down. I'm my own agent for now, but I've got a lawyer to look over the contract." He slipped a card into Paul's hand. "He'll handle the important stuff."

"Very good." Paul chuckled. "If you put the same amount of emotion into my film as you are in this relationship you've got going with Zayn, then we'll all be fine." He nodded to Kris. "Speaking of Zayn, you'd better run to catch up with him."

"What? Huh?" Kris glanced over his shoulder at Zayn's retreating form. He turned his attention back to Paul. "Sorry. That was unprofessional. I promise while I'm on set, the film will be my top priority."

"As much as it pains me to say this, guys and girls are a dime a dozen in this business. I like Zayn. He's good people, but you've got to know what you want. You'll meet lots of people and have lots of relationships." Paul clapped Kris on the shoulder. "It'll be fine."

"You did know I was in porn, right? This will be my first official crossover film." Kris stood firm. If Zayn wanted to hightail it out of there, then fine. He had business to deal with before he chased his agent, friend…whatever.

"I did. I think it's cool that you're making the move. You deserve to be happy." Paul widened his stance and folded his arms. "You're going to have to understand that your job will turn people off, but it'll also make others rally for you. I can't wait to see what you do. You're a dynamic actor. As for the situation with Zayn…give him time. He's got issues, but not necessarily with you. Eli fucked him over good. If you're using him to move up the food chain, he'll know and won't put up with the bullshit."

"He's explained that. My question was how he felt about me and why he wanted to help me. I'm not trying to be ungrateful, but I've never had someone care. It's a long story." Kris shook his head. "Suffice it to say, I had to make all my own breaks until he came along. I like that he's my support, but I also don't want him to feel that he has to save me."

"Give him time. Show him you're not another dick trying to fuck his way to the top and you'll be fine. Might not end up with him, but you'll know where you stand and will be better for the experience." Paul shook his hand once more. "I'll plan on seeing you on set next week. Congrats, and memorize those lines."

"I will." Kris smiled, then turned on his heel and hurried after Zayn. They'd ridden together, so unless Zayn took a taxi, he should still be somewhere around. He burst through the front doors of the building and raced into the parking lot. "Zayn?"

Shit. He didn't see his friend anywhere. "Zayn? Come on." He detoured past his car and stopped. Zayn sat on the trunk of the car. "There you are," Kris said and stopped to catch his breath. "I'm sorry."

"Sorry?" Zayn rested his elbows on his knees and clasped his hands together. "We've got to get a few things straight. I've got a job to do. I've been asked to cast three major motion pictures in the next two months. You've now got two acting jobs which should take you roughly that long."

Kris listened carefully to everything Zayn said. He'd screwed up by blowing his top back in the building. Keeping cool now and waiting would be his best bet for getting back into Zayn's good graces.

"Since you're going straight, you can't go off all moody and possessive like that. You've got to make the right impression." Zayn shook his head. "Paul won't care, but others will."

"I know."

"You—you do?" Zayn's eyes widened. "Then why did you act like a fucking dick in there?"

Kris debated his answer. He needed to be perfectly honest, but not go off. He wanted Zayn to be more than his friend. "There are a few things about me you need to understand. Talking in a parking lot won't help. Please, let me buy you dinner and we'll take it back to my condo. I'll tell you anything you want to know."

"Kris?" Zayn tipped his head to the side. "But..."

"The bottom line is that I like you. I want to be more than friends with you. Ripping our clothes off and having sex all night long, then holding each other, yeah. I want to do it." Kris hooked his fingers into his jeans pockets. "When I made that last picture with Gerry, I focused on you. Because of you, I got into character. I imagined you in his place. I want to be with you, but I'm getting the feeling *you* don't want to be with *me*. I'm not interested in being a rung on the ladder or anything like that. I want to see where this will go between us. If the next two months mean we fall apart, then we do. I'm willing to take that risk."

Zayn stared at him, but didn't say anything.

"I'll take you back to the condo and you can decide what you want to do from there. Pizza's on me if you're interested." Kris fished his keys from his pants pocket, then unlocked the car. "Ready?"

Zayn slid off the trunk, then walked over to the passenger door. "I am." He plopped onto the passenger seat.

Kris sighed and slid behind the wheel of the car. Neither of them spoke for the entire ride back to the condo. Once he parked, Kris dialed his favorite pizza pub. "What would you like on the pizza?"

"Mushrooms," Zayn replied.

"Anything else?"

"I'm good with whatever you want." Zayn walked into the condo and knelt next to the dog.

Kris turned his back on his friend and finished his order. He slid his phone back into his pocket, then joined his dog and Zayn in the condo. "I've got wine. Want some? It's a nice red. I had a bottle of it at a party. I liked it." He was babbling. "Sorry."

"You say you're sorry a lot." Zayn joined Kris in the kitchen. "I'd love a glass."

Kris poured the wine, then dumped dog food into Nugent's bowl. He placed the bowl on the floor. "Bottoms up."

"You don't have your glass yet." Zayn picked up both wine goblets. "Congratulations on the role and here's to a great career with your clothes on."

"Here, here." Kris clinked glasses with Zayn. "Thanks."

"I said you'd be great. You were. You deserve the part." Zayn smiled. He sipped the wine, then toyed with the stem of the drinkware. "I've been thinking about what you said. Who hurt you? Someone, somewhere really did a number on you."

"You have no idea," Kris muttered.

"I know. That's why I'm trying to talk to you. Let me in." Zayn put his glass on the counter, then gathered Kris in his arms. "I'm a lousy boyfriend, but I'm a good listener. I care about you. I don't know how to tell you exactly how I feel. I've been hurt and my head says to hold back, but my heart wants to plunge headlong into something with you."

Kris stared into Zayn's eyes. A man could get lost in those eyes. "I'm game." Crap. He sounded so...frat boy-ish.

"Fuck me." Zayn grasped Kris' hands and yanked him down the hall to the bedroom. "Right now."

"Zayn?" He wasn't saying no, but he also wasn't sure what changed Zayn's mind.

"Can't wait." Zayn shoved Kris onto the bed and opened Kris' pants. He freed Kris' cock from the denim. "I need this." He tugged on Kris' pants.

Kris planted his feet on the floor to aid Zayn's enthusiasm. He preferred to take control, but allowing Zayn to have the lead was sexy.

"Condoms?" Zayn shucked his own pants and wrapped his hand around his cock. He hadn't even removed his shirt.

"Nightstand." Kris reached for the piece of furniture, but Zayn batted his hand out of the way.

Zayn retrieved the rubber and a bottle of lube. He sheathed Kris and dribbled the clear liquid all over Kris' cock. "I can't wait."

"Slow. You're not going to kiss me?" Kris asked.

"Next time." Zayn yanked his shirt up over his head, then climbed onto Kris' lap. A tiny barbell twinkled in Zayn's right nipple. "I've been thinking about this all day." He lined Kris' dick up with his hole.

"Slow down. You'll hurt yourself." Kris grasped Zayn's hips and took over. He eased Zayn down onto his shaft, giving Zayn time to adjust to the invasion in his ass. Plus, he wanted to take a gander at that piercing. He'd seen plenty of metal in body parts before, but he wouldn't have pegged Zayn for the piercing type—a tattoo, maybe, but not a piercing. The thin bar of metal in his nipple was sexy.

"Hot damn, that feels good. I love the burn." Zayn closed his eyes. His nipples beaded and he tipped his head back. "Wow." The change in position put more emphasis on his chest and the piercing.

"I like being inside you." Kris moved his lover up and down on his cock, massaging every inch of Zayn from the inside out.

"Fuck." Zayn curled forward and rested his forehead against Kris'. "I lied. I want to kiss you." He bit Kris' bottom lip.

When he looked into Kris' eyes, Kris saw forever. Crazy, since this was their first time and they hadn't known each other long, but he could see himself settling down with a man like Zayn.

"Oh, God," Zayn bit out. He leaned back and met Kris thrust for thrust.

Within seconds, the tingles in Kris' belly shot around his body. His legs trembled and his skin heated. "I'm close," he announced.

"Me too." Zayn shivered. He fisted his cock, stroking himself in time with Kris' thrusts. Another shiver wracked his body. "Fuck." A ribbon of cum shot across Kris' T-shirt. Zayn opened his eyes and stared at Kris.

"Jesus." Kris tensed. The orgasm that had built in his groin released. He'd been out of practice and forgotten how a climax felt while making love, not a porn film. He gathered Zayn in his arms and held him to his chest. "That was good."

"You can talk?" Zayn panted. "My brain is mush."

"Mine is too." Truth be told, he wasn't sure how he'd formed a complete sentence. He held Zayn and grinned to himself. They'd fucked. Better than he'd imagined. He never wanted to leave the bed. Eventually the world would intrude on their good feelings, but he wanted the moment to last as long as possible.

"What's that?" Zayn wriggled out of Kris' arms. "I heard a bell."

The dog barked, then ran into the bedroom.

Kris froze. Shit. "The pizza." He'd gotten so wrapped up in being with Zayn that he'd lost all track of time.

Zayn laughed. "We forgot about it." He slid off Kris' lap. "Better get it."

"With jizz on my shirt and my pants around my ankles? Shout out there and tell him we'll be right there." Kris fumbled to his feet and yanked off his shirt. "Please?"

"Will do." Zayn yanked his pants up. Shirtless, he darted from the room.

Kris fumbled through the dresser drawer for a pair of sleep pants. He dressed in the soft cotton, then retrieved a new shirt from the middle drawer. When he rounded the corner, Zayn already had the pizza on the table. Nugent stood beside him, tail wagging and begging for a slice of the pie.

"Aren't you cute, begging?" Kris ambled into the room. "You paid? This was my treat."

Zayn shrugged. "No problem. It's a party. We're celebrating." He handed over the slice of pizza on one of Kris' paper plates. "I saw these on the counter. Here. Eat up, handsome actor man."

He stared at Zayn. Since the ride home, he wasn't sure what had happened, but his friend had changed. "I'll bite. All the sudden you want to have sex with me and you're being nicer. No shitting, are you interested in me? Not just for a project or something? I'm not trying to be a bitch, but I need to know."

Zayn plated another slice of pizza, then tore a chunk of cheese off and handed it to the dog. He nodded to the chair, then sat opposite Kris. "I've been thinking about what happened. I've been hot and cold with you. I tried to say it was because you didn't want me to get close, but there's more to it than that, because you did want me to get close to you. This is partially on my shoulders. I couldn't decide if I wanted to help you because it made me feel good, because I wanted to see you succeed or because I do have a vested interest."

Kris toyed with the edge of the plate. He wasn't going to blurt anything out now. No fucking way.

"I'm done keeping these walls up around me. I want to be with someone—you. I've got stuff I have to do in my life, like work on other movies, but I want to help you. You've got that spark. You're a wild card right now, but you're so much more. I dream about being with you, want to feel your arms around me and even though it's happening so fast, I'm ready to make the change." Zayn smiled. "Really."

"I'm sorry." Kris paused. He needed to compose his thoughts. If he said the wrong thing, he'd sound like an idiot and that was the last thing he wanted to do.

"Wait, what?" Zayn's smile melted. "I missed something."

"I needed a chance to think. First, I'm sorry I flew off the handle at the studio. That wasn't cool. I damaged your cred and mine." In other sticky situations, he didn't meet the other person's gaze. This time was different. He owed Zayn more than just a look. "Really."

"Well, you learned from the situation and are going to move forward accordingly. I'm not mad." Zayn bit into his pizza and moaned. "This is so good. I need to write down the number to this pizza house."

Kris tugged more cheese from the slice. He'd kept so much locked inside. The other relationships he'd been in weren't deep. The guys wanted sex or a job. Zayn wasn't expecting either. If he opened up, he'd feel better. Part of him wanted to stay closed off. The rest of him needed to let someone else into his private hell.

"You look like you're in La-La land." Zayn tapped Kris' plate. "Are you in there?"

"I'm staring at your piercing. Wouldn't have thought you'd have one. I've got the tats, but no piercings."

"Oh, that." Zayn shrugged. "I did it to impress a guy but the dick didn't end up liking it. To piss him off, I kept it in. It's a part of me now. Why the tats? Credibility?"

"No. They all have meaning." He lifted his right shirtsleeve. "The black horse is a dark horse—I'll succeed but you won't expect it. I've got the *Superman* 'S' on my left arm and my initials on the back of my neck so I never forget who I am." The relationship was new and fragile, but Kris decided in that moment that he needed to tell his story. "Answer me something. If you knew something raw about someone, would you still want to be with them?"

"Um…depends. Are you keeping something from me?" Zayn chewed more of the pizza, then sipped the wine from his glass. "I'm not going to run away. Hit me with it."

Kris dropped his hands into his lap and sighed. "I don't have a disease or anything. I keep that up because I don't want to get sick. Can't work if I'm sick."

"Okay." Zayn reached across the table. "What is it then?"

The words melted away. Christ. He needed strength. He'd kept this secret for so long. Kris met Zayn's gaze again and found strength. "I wasn't completely honest about my reasons for getting into porn. Yes, I was trying to get regular acting jobs and waiting tables, but there's more to it."

"You're a closet nympho?" Zayn chuckled. "Bad joke. Sorry. It's what I do when I'm stressed—I make stupid jokes. Ignore me."

"I wish it was that simple." Kris' knee bounced and his stomach knotted. "When I was thirteen, I went with my family to a get-together. You know, one of those big family things where no one is watching the kids, but you're all safe? One of those." He grasped Zayn's hand. "Everything wasn't all right, though." He shook his head. He couldn't do this. Couldn't go through with telling his secret.

"What happened?" Zayn let go of Kris' hand and rounded the table. He knelt at Kris' feet. "Talk. I'm not going anywhere."

"It's not that easy." His eyes burned. Shit. He was going to cry. The memories rushed back into his head. "It was my mother." His stomach churned. If he wasn't careful, he'd throw up.

"Okay. Hey." Zayn rose up on his knees and wrapped his arms around Kris' waist. "When you're ready, I'm here."

He dragged a couple of long breaths into his lungs and let them out slowly. He needed to calm down. But how? Hell, he was on the verge of disclosing something he'd held on to for more than twelve years. No, it was time. He balled his fists and allowed the words to come.

"An Easter party...at my grandmother's. I hadn't come out yet, but my parents knew I was gay. Dad said he had an inkling. He supported me and said to behave, but if I had questions, he'd answer them." Kris gasped for air. "Mom wasn't so...approving."

"Parents know sometimes faster than we figure it out. Mine knew, too, but it was my father who had the fit. He said I was gay because it was cool." Zayn smoothed his hands along Kris' chest, up to his neck then cupped Kris' jaw in both hands. "I like dick and I'm not going to change who I am."

Kris could still hear his father's voice in his head. *Kiss a boy. Find out if you like it as much as you think, but be mindful. Not everyone will accept you.* He appreciated what his father had said. He'd kissed a boy, really liked it and kissed another one. Those memories remained sweet in his mind. The other memories weren't so sweet.

A dull ache started behind his eyes. He blinked back the tears threatening to fall. When he closed his eyes, he saw the moment all over again. His ass puckered and his chest ached. "At the party, my mother decided to make an example out of me. She embarrassed me in front of my cousins and told them I wasn't interested in girls. She said I was sick in the head and needed straightened out." His throat hurt, but he pushed forward. "She told my uncle, her brother, to do something about me. I was thirteen." The tears fell. *Fuck.* He shivered. Admitting this truth was harder than he'd ever thought.

Zayn didn't say a word. He didn't shy away or wince. Instead, he swiped his thumb along Kris' cheek.

"He took me into a room and…" His voice cracked. "He was my first."

"Oh my God." Zayn threw his arms around Kris. "I'm so sorry. Honey."

"He told me I was worthless," Kris bit out. "Said I had a disease and needed fixed…like I was a cat."

"No." Zayn rested his forehead against Kris'. "That's not true. You can't fix who you are. I like you this way because it's you."

Hearing those words comforted him almost as much Zayn's arms around him. Kris gulped for air. "After that, I had to sit with everyone at the dinner table and face them. He and my mother glared at me the entire time. I couldn't talk about it—I wanted to, especially to my dad. I started talking a couple of times, but couldn't finish. The last time I tried to say something to my father, my mother burst into the room and claimed I was lying. Why would I lie about that?"

"Because she knew she was wrong," Zayn murmured. "People like to hide when they know they've done something they shouldn't. I'd be willing to bet she was so angry about your decision that even though she knew the truth, she convinced herself her version was the correct one."

Sounded about right. For the remainder of his time at home, his mother had dropped hints that his sexuality was wrong. She probably did believe her version of the truth. God knew she hadn't allowed the subject to go away. "My mother waited until my father went to work and allowed my uncle to come over. They were fixing me, they said. Over and over." He bit back bile. "Made me feel worthless. Told me I was worthless. I believed them. Why would someone do that to a kid, much less a confused teenager?"

"You're not worthless. That's garbage." Zayn shook his head. "They knew you couldn't and wouldn't talk about what happened. They are the worthless ones."

Somehow he still didn't believe what Zayn said. He pressed on in order to finish the story.

"What did you do?" Zayn asked. "How'd you get away from it?"

"School and drama club were my ways to escape. The theater teacher asked me over and over why I didn't want to go home. Dad thought I was being rebellious. I wanted to say something. I wanted anyone to hear what had happened, but even when I tried to say something, I was told I was being dramatic. I was trying to get attention. You can't fake that shit."

"No, you can't."

"I hated myself. There weren't enough plays or clubs or anything else enough to block out those memories. Once I got my license, I used to drive three towns over and club at this funky place. It was fun at the time, but looking back I never should've been there." He closed his eyes. The drinking, the clubbing and all those one-night stands didn't dull the pain. They made the pain worse and cut deeper. "I came to California to escape my problems, but they followed me. I didn't get into the big time right away and believed the crap I'd been told. I was worthless and everyone else seemed to know. When I was introduced to porn, I jumped. I could kill the demons inside me and encourage the crappy ass feelings."

"What made you change your mind?"

"I didn't want to hurt any longer." Kris sighed and wriggled from Zayn's grasp. He walked away from the table. He needed air. God. He'd let his secret out. Zayn could do anything now. He thrust both hands into his hair. "I still don't believe I'm a worthy guy. I can act, but it's because I've been hiding this shit for more than fifteen years. I got tired of the mask." He shook his head. "I'm just tired."

"You don't have to be tired alone." Zayn eased up behind him and wrapped his arms around Kris. "I won't let you."

"I kept the façade up because it's easier. No one has to know what I'm going through and can see the crap. It makes me angry and kept me from getting close to people. That's why I lashed out at you. I can't understand why you're here. I don't deserve this." As much as he wanted to be free of Zayn, he needed to hold tight.

"Slow down, handsome." Zayn turned Kris around in his embrace. "Getting all of that out has to be tough. I'm sure you're hurting." He kissed Kris' nose, then his lips. "I know you can't change the past, but I'm not going anywhere. Your past is just that—old news. This is our time and our situation. I'm falling for the guy right here with me."

"You're crazy."

"And that's the frustration talking." Zayn smiled. "You're more than your past and soon you'll see it. You want to believe and you can see that light at the end, but it's going to take some time. I've got lots of time." He placed his fingers over Kris' lips. "It's hard, but trust me. Please?"

Kris hesitated. This was what he wanted—a man to care about him despite the crap he'd been through. Zayn wanted to be that person. Zayn had faith in him and refused to allow him to perform in porn.

"Okay." Kris nodded. More tears streamed down his cheeks. Things weren't permanent between him and Zayn, but he had someone on his side. He also had a chance to make his life more than the dirty movies.

"Follow your heart. I'm right here beside you, pushing you to live your dream." Zayn grinned. He cried too. "You bring out the best in me and make me all emotional. I like it."

"I like you too." Kris closed his eyes. He could do this. He could move forward. Yes, he had Zayn as his cheerleader, but he was strong enough to make his dreams work.

"You're my wild card and I'm betting everything on you." Zayn tugged Kris to his knees. "We've left someone out." He hugged the dog between their bodies. "Nugent wanted to be a part of this. He's proud of you too."

"Stay tonight." Kris hugged them both, then kissed Zayn on the lips. "Stay with me."

"I'm not going anywhere." Zayn let go of the dog, then glanced over Kris' shoulder. "But...we might have to do some cleaning."

"You want to have sex on the floor?" Kris asked.

"No, the dog dragged the pizza off the table and you've got red sauce on the carpet." Zayn sighed and chuckled. "You've got something to get stains out of the flooring?"

"I do." Kris laughed along with Zayn. Life wouldn't be boring with Zayn and Nugent. He sat on his rump on the floor. In the space of two days, his life had turned around. So much had happened. He still wasn't thrilled about his past, but he was ready to embrace the future and holy crap, what a future he had ahead of him—two movies and a new direction in his life. *Hell, yeah.*

Chapter Seven

Zayn spent the night as well as the rest of the weekend with Kris. Each moment they were together, he learned more about his friend. The revelations Kris had mentioned didn't scare him off the way Kris must've thought. Everyone had scars and ghosts in their past. God knew he'd done things he wasn't proud to admit.

He stood outside the condo with Kris. "So, you're going on location. This is the first time, right?"

"Location where it's not within two hours of home." Kris scrubbed his hand along the back of his neck. "I'm excited, but I'm scared. I know my lines—but what if I screw up?"

"What happened when you screwed up on the porn sets?" Zayn grasped Kris' shoulders. "I'm being serious. Did they laugh and tell you to go? No. They reset the scene and edited out the goof."

"True." Kris fidgeted beside the car. "What about Nugent? I just got him. I can't leave him." He groaned. "I can't put him in one of those tiny trailers."

"I'll take care of him. Give me a key." Zayn massaged his boyfriend's tense muscles. "Come on. You trust me enough to sleep with me. Nugent likes me and he trusts me."

Kris chuckled. Although Zayn couldn't see his eyes because of the dark sunglasses, he knew that smile. "Are you my boyfriend? I mean, high school–sounding crap aside, what exactly are we to each other?"

"Far as I'm concerned, you're my boyfriend. I'm quite fond of you." Zayn embraced his lover right there in front of anyone who happened to be outside on the street. "I let you fuck my ass six times this weekend and loved every moment of it. I'd like to do it again right now, but if you don't get going soon, you'll be late for filming."

"It's wardrobe stuff, then some practice to block out exactly where they want us." Kris shrugged. "I'd rather have sex too."

"We've got a good thing going."

"It'll seem like forever until I get to see you." Kris rested his forehead against Zayn's. "I've got the extra key under the mat and I'll write down the security code. He grabbed Zayn's hand and scribbled five numbers. "There. Take care of Nuge and don't totally forget about me."

"You've got your phone and laptop. You'll have Wi-Fi because they'll need it to send the film back to the main studio. Email me or call me. Hell, call me every night."

"You're sure? Every night?" Kris grasped Zayn's hands. "Cool. Thank you."

"Get going. Paul won't like you being late on the first day." Zayn kissed him again. "I'll get the key while you're getting in the car, then you can go." He turned on his heel and hurried over to where Kris had said the key would be. He found the shiny bit of brass, then rushed back to the car. Kris sat behind the wheel.

"I'm going to do this. I'm an actor." He grinned at Zayn. "I'm an actor."

"Don't get a big head about it, hunk." He leaned in the window and kissed Kris one more time. "Show 'em what you're made of."

He waited until Kris had backed down the driveway, drove down the street and disappeared around the corner before he went back inside. The condo was nice, but not quite home without Kris there. Odd, since they'd only been together for a short period of time. But he'd grown quite fond of Kris. He loved Nugent too. He'd never considered himself a dog person until he'd met Kris and Nugent.

"Just you and me, buddy." He closed the front door, then sat on the floor with the dog. Nugent flopped down beside him, but wasn't his usual happy self. "I miss him too."

He sighed. Kris was doing what he loved and finally getting the chance to show he could act. So why was Zayn so down? He needed to go to work at the studios and had things to do, but he wanted to be with Kris at night. Maybe it was the magic of being with the porn star or the rush of finding someone who wasn't afraid to be honest, but he'd fallen in love with Kris.

"Two weeks, plus three days of costuming and other stuff." He petted the dog's head. "You've got me until he gets back. We're a team."

An hour later, Zayn combed his hair and adjusted his shirt. He'd been asked to join the creative team on one of the big-budget action movies. The director and producer wanted to fill the principle roles with seasoned actors, but hadn't found the right people. As usual, he was expected to find the right fits and in no time.

He jiggled Nugent's leash. "Want to go with me?"

Nugent surged to Zayn's side. His tail swished wildly and he practically vibrated. Zayn attached the leash to Nugent's collar, then wrapped the handle end around his wrist. "Good boy." He slung his messenger bag over his shoulder and headed out of the condo.

Within minutes, he'd locked the front door and settled behind the wheel of his car. He backed down the drive and noticed the neighbor watching him. Normally he'd have flipped the guy the bird, but he didn't trust Henry. Something about the guy screamed unhinged. Then again, anyone who would leave a dog tied out with no food or water for days on end wasn't quite right. Zayn drove across town to the studio.

A line had formed beside the main building. Guys of all shapes, races and builds were in the queue to read for him. He groaned. Shit.

"I thought they were on the prowl for seasoned actors," he mumbled to Nugent. Zayn parked and gathered up the dog's leash and his things, then went into the lobby.

"Hey." Paul stopped Zayn. "You're working on the action flick?"

"Casting, yes."

"Who is this guy?"

"Kris' dog. I'm doggy-sitting." Zayn knelt beside Nugent. "Nugent. He's very well behaved."

"Makes you look tough with your pittie—er, Kris' dog." Paul folded his arms. "He's working out. Follows directions well and doesn't argue—so far. He might turn into a diva. I'm hoping not. I like working with him."

"Speaking of working, why are you here? I thought your movie was independent." Zayn stood. He offered Nugent a treat. "Working on a side project?"

"The studio offered to pay for my horror movie. Since I have Lyndsay Turlington in the flick, they want to promote her. It works out. I'm still doing a lot of hand-held camera work, but I get better security out of the deal and better food for the cast."

"Cool."

"I came up here to get some of the paperwork turned in. I've got Cleve doing the blocking for the first few scenes." Paul grinned. "Take this. If you want on the set to visit your boy, this'll get you there."

"My own pass. Cool." Zayn bit back a chuckle. He'd been given carte blanche access to so many sets, he'd forgotten what it was like to actually need a special pass. "Thanks."

"I'm out." Paul waved, then strolled away.

"I'm late," Zayn muttered. He walked the dog to the assigned committee room. "Sorry." He took his spot next to the director. Nugent flopped onto the floor at Zayn's feet. For being abused and neglected, the dog took to commands well. Zayn slipped his shoe off and rubbed the canine's belly. "Okay, so you've got five candidates, correct?"

Zayn flipped through the dossiers on the different actors. He'd cast each of the actors, save for one, in different motion pictures. Choosing one would be difficult.

Four hours and five auditions later, Zayn stretched. "I need a few. I'm taking Nugent to the gardens for a walk so I can think over my choices."

Nugent snorted, then trotted alongside Zayn to the courtyard. He knew damn well who he thought would be the best fit for the part. The auditions had all gone well, but only one really stood out. The walk was more for Nugent's benefit than a proper actor selection. On the second lap around the courtyard, Zayn checked the messages on his phone. The icon for text messages flashed. He pressed the correct buttons and three pictures loaded onto the screen—all of Kris.

Kris grinned in front of a woody area, with the caption, *getting' dirty, wish it was with you.*

Yeah, he wished he was there too.

The second photo featured Kris frowning and pointing to the occupancy sign on his trailer. *Occupants = 1. No fair.*

Zayn chuckled. Only Kris would think a single-person trailer was unfair.

The final picture showed Kris pointing to his heart. *I miss you.*

"I miss you, too, you big goof." God, the nights were going to be long. He knew better than to rush over to the set on the first day. Kris still had to gel with his castmates and an intrusion like Zayn and Nugent wouldn't help.

Zayn snapped a photo of himself and the dog, then typed a return message.

Having fun, but wish you were here. Do a great job so you can get a bigger trailer next time.

He sent the message, then headed back to the conference room. Time to get his own job done.

* * * *

Over the next seven days, Zayn spent most of the time at the different studios. He cast fifteen roles in two movies. When he could bring Nugent along, he did. If he couldn't, he left the canine in the condo. He battled guilt at leaving the dog alone. As soon as he could leave, he rushed home to the pet.

He'd called Kris each night. The first six nights, Kris talked for a couple of hours, but the night before hadn't lasted as long. Paul had wanted to shoot the night scenes before the rains came. They wouldn't be able to talk that night because of more filming.

Zayn stretched out on the bed with his laptop on his belly. Nugent snored beside him, where Kris should've been lying. He flipped through the texted images from Kris. At least his boyfriend appeared to be having a good time.

He petted the dog and tried to focus on prep work for the next set of auditions. His phone rang and without looking at the ID, he answered. "Kris?"

"Not Kris — whoever that is. It's Eli."

Zayn's stomach soured. He knew the moment he heard Eli's voice who the caller happened to be and didn't want to talk with his ex. "I thought you lost my number. Please do." Zayn hung up on his ex-boyfriend. Why in the hell did Eli want him? Probably for a role.

The phone rang again, but this time he checked the number. Same as the last time. Eli. *Fuck no.* He turned the phone over to quiet the ringing. He couldn't turn the sound totally off in case Kris did call.

When he attempted to read through the parts the actors would be reading the next day, his phone rang ten more times and all Eli. *What the fuck?* He gritted his teeth. Although he had nothing to say to his ex-boyfriend, he wanted the calls to stop.

Zayn answered the next call. "What do you want?"

"Is that any way to speak to the love of your life?" Eli asked.

Zayn pinched the bridge of his nose. *Love of my life.* "You used to be, but you dicked me over. Get on with your...why you called. I'm busy."

"Doing what? Or whom?"

"That's not your business," Zayn snapped.

"If he was that good, you wouldn't be able to answer the phone."

"You called me a total of fourteen times. It's annoying. Get to the point." Zayn massaged his temple. The man knew how to push buttons.

"Fine. I've been asked to read for a part in *Fourth of July*. It's a tiny part—someone's boyfriend—but it's an ensemble cast and I really want in it."

"Okay? Not seeing where I come in." Zayn closed his laptop. He knew exactly what Eli wanted. He'd been asked to help cast the picture. Eli hadn't shown up on any of his lists.

"You're the casting director. You're in charge of putting people who belong in the film in it. I'm not on your list, I'm sure, but I can do this part," Eli begged. "Come on. For old time's sake. You know you want me in this."

"No, I don't," Zayn said flatly. Hell could freeze over, but he refused to put Eli in one of his movies.

"So you'll bust your ass to put porn boy in a movie, but not me?"

"Porn boy?" Zayn stopped from lashing out at his ex. He didn't want to engage the prick, but damn it, Eli had no business making fun of Kris.

"Yeah, I know about him. Everyone does. You're his bitch, aren't you?"

"Define everyone," Zayn growled.

"You're getting pissy. That's one sign," Eli said. "Why? Why would you work so hard to get that...guy a role, but not me? God knows I'm hotter. He's all…gross. He looks like he'd do porn. Too many muscles. Does he eat nothing but protein powder?"

"You're a dick." Zayn pounded his fist on the mattress. "Let's cut to the chase. You want a role and you're expecting me to put you in that role, correct?"

"Yes."

"No."

"No?" Eli grunted. "You don't get to tell me no."

"You heard me. If you're not on the list, then you didn't make the cut that gets to audition in front of me. I'm sorry for your luck. Honestly, though, I'm glad. Even the smallest roles in that film would be above your acting abilities. You couldn't act like a gentleman enough to be honest with me and you sure as hell couldn't hide your cheating on me. I'm sorry, but the role has been filled."

"By *him*?"

"No." Zayn didn't give Eli a chance to answer or to call back. He switched the ringer to silence, then fired off a text to Kris explaining that the ringer wasn't working and to text if he wanted to talk.

"The guy is a dick," Zayn said and petted Nugent. "Why I got involved with him is beyond me. I must've been crazy."

Five minutes later, he shut down the laptop and switched off the light. The auditions in the morning would take most of the day, easily, and he needed to get some sleep. The phone lit up the room, startling Zayn. He flipped the device around. A text—from Kris.

You okay? That text seemed pissy. Call me?

Zayn sighed. This was one phone conversation he *wanted* to have. He dialed his boyfriend's number. After one ring, Kris answered.

"Hi. How is everything? Is Nugent okay?" Kris asked.

"He's fine. To keep things somewhat normal for him, I stay over at your place. He sleeps in your spot on the bed. Make a note, we need to get a bigger bed." Zayn laughed. "King-sized should do."

"He'll be spoiled by the time I get home." Kris chuckled. "I'm glad, though. How about you? You sounded stressed in that text."

"A little. It's been a rough day." Zayn snuggled in the blankets. "If you've got time to talk, tell me about your day so I forget mine."

"I've got ten minutes—but I can make those ten minutes last a long time."

"Do it," Zayn said. "I need you."

"I need you too." Kris muttered something Zayn couldn't hear, then he came back on the line. "I had to go into my trailer. It's raining again and Paul's having a fit. He wanted some rain, but not three straight days. We've filmed all the indoors stuff we can and even some of the rainy scene stuff, but we need dry days to finish."

"That happens sometimes."

"They made me wear this thick makeup that covers my tattoos. My neck feels all crusty by the end of the shooting day. I understand why they want them covered, but it's a mess."

Zayn crossed his ankles and sighed. This was the kind of conversation he liked—one where they could talk shop without an argument.

"I keep thinking of ways to make the film more sexual. Guess I'm in a rut," Kris said and laughed. "Can't get sex off the brain."

"Then tell me your ideas. It'll get it out of your head." Zayn slid one hand beneath the blankets and massaged the growing bulge in his underwear. "I won't lie. I'm here because of the dog, but I'm also in your bed because it smells like you."

"You like the way I smell?" Kris asked. His voice dropped an octave.

"I do."

"Then I don't want to talk about the movie. I want to talk about what I want to do when I get home." Kris groaned. "I won't tell you when I'm coming. I'll walk in and surprise you, but you'd be asleep."

"Why would I be asleep?" He rubbed his cock through the cotton of his shorts. "Can't wait to see you." He liked where this was going, though.

"You'd be asleep because you've been waiting up for me and I'm late. Filming went long. When I get home, I'd lock the door and surprise you. I'll crawl on top of you, kissing all your exposed skin."

"I'd be waiting naked," Zayn replied. He shoved his hand underneath the elastic of his underwear. "My surprise to you."

"I like it." Another groan. "I'd nip your neck, feeling your pulse under my lips. It's sexy. You wake up and wrap your arms around me. Your cock is already hard and it's jabbing into my belly, but I don't care."

"Feels good." He propped the phone up on the pillow and shoved both hands down his underwear. He eased the cotton down his hips, exposing himself. Free of the garment, he wrapped both hands around his dick. "I'm hard for you."

"You want my cock in your ass. You crave me."

"Babe, I do." He stroked himself, loving the feel of his hands on his body and wishing they were really Kris touching him. He shivered. "Never had phone sex before, but I love it."

"You bet your ass you do," Kris said. "Touch your hole. Tell me how it feels."

"Lonely." He whimpered as he caressed his asshole. "I'd rather you be here."

"I want to be. I miss your ass."

Zayn closed his eyes and tapped his hole with his middle finger. At the same time, he stroked himself. His body heated and his skin sizzled. He grunted and increased the pressure around his cock. He kicked the blankets off as best he could to keep from jizzing all over the bedding.

"I'm so close," he panted. "I want to come."

"Do you?" Kris' question came out like a tease and was probably meant to.

"God, I need to." His strokes damn near broke his dick off. He tensed and dug his feet into the mattress. He trembled.

"Come for me. I want to hear it. Moan."

He didn't need much coaxing. Zayn groaned. From deep in his being, the climax took over. "Oh, fucking hell." He gritted his teeth and yanked hard on his dick. Cum spurted onto his belly in a hot rope. "Oh my God."

"Sounds like heaven," Kris murmured. "I can see you in my mind and you're hot as hell."

His thoughts blurred together. Nothing mattered except being in the moment with Kris. He gasped for breath and opened his eyes. The room spun. Once everything settled a bit, he sighed. "You're good with ten minutes."

"Took me a little longer than ten minutes, but you're welcome." Kris chuckled. "While you were coming apart, Paul gave us the rest of the night off. The rain isn't stopping like he thought."

"Oh." He sagged against the sheets. "I'm glad you're not late. I would hate to be the reason you're in trouble." He stared at the ceiling. "It's not like me to lose myself in someone like this, but I'm glad. I like you."

"I like you too. Wish I was there, since you're in my bed. I hate this one. It's lumpy."

"They all are." But they could have a good time working out the lumps together.

"I've got to go. Paul just bellowed. Good night, Zayn. Take care of my dog."

"He's happily snoring beside me." Zayn closed his eyes again. The smell of Kris' cologne on the sheets comforted him. "See you in what, a week?"

"A week. Can't wait. Until then, good night."

"Good night, babe." Zayn disconnected the call and smiled to himself. Things weren't set in stone, but he was truly head over heels for Kris. The words 'I love you' teetered on the tip of his tongue. He fumbled for his shirt on the floor and wiped the cum off his belly. He'd clean the shirt in the morning. He snuggled in the sheets and draped an arm across the dog's middle. His thoughts filled with Kris and their hot time as he fell asleep.

* * * *

Zayn woke in the morning feeling better than he had in a long time. He showered, shaved and dressed, then attached the leash to Nugent's collar. He headed to the studio to help cast a kids' movie. Kid movies weren't his thing, but he'd been asked to help with the adults on the film. Having Nugent with him eased a bit of his loneliness and made him feel closer to Kris. Silly, but he'd fallen for the dog too.

He sat through what seemed like endless auditions by adults who had no idea how to interact with children. A handful were good, but not the right build wanted for the various parts. He made notes and suggestions to the producers. The director shared his vision for the film. Thankfully, what Zayn wanted matched with the director's ideas.

"That's it," the producer finally said. "I've seen enough this morning. I need a break. What time is it?"

"Past three," one of the assistants said.

"Christ. I need a cigarette." The producer strolled out of the room, leaving Zayn alone with Dylan, the director.

"You got a new dog?" Dylan petted Nugent. "He's cute. Dangerous, but cute."

"He's a big cuddle bug." Zayn slid his notes over to Dylan. "I've got these three candidates for the female lead. Any of them would be good, but she would be best." He tapped the paper. "The other two are good, though."

"What about the male lead? He's got to interact with the kids more."

"Well, none of them are exactly what you want. Plain and simple, none of the guys fit the bill. They aren't tall or whatever. The one that will do what is best is actually this guy." He pointed to one of the names. "He has kids, so can handle them. He's not tall, but he's strong and has a large presence on the screen. I've seen him work before and he can do the part—if you're willing to give him the chance."

"Another one of your wild cards?" Dylan asked. He wrote down the name. "I'll bring him in tomorrow, but I see your point. Sometimes the right person for the role isn't the person we expect, but he or she is perfect once they give the performance."

"I aim to please and yes, you're correct. We done? I need to take Nugent for a walk." When Zayn stood, the dog joined him.

"How about I walk with you?" Dylan pushed his chair in. "I've been wanting to talk to you about something."

"Did Eli contact you?" Son of bitch, the punk probably did. "He wants in on your July film. He's not right for it, but he's pushy."

"No, that's not what I wanted to talk about," Dylan replied. "Well, no, actually he called my office. My receptionist told him I wasn't accepting any other outside auditions. He sent me an email with his audition reel too. I deleted it. That kind of crazy is *not* what I want in the film he wants to do."

"I'm sorry. He was a mistake and I never should've…" Zayn pushed the doors open to the courtyard behind the studio. He loved to wander the lot to see which films were in production, but with a dog he couldn't wander without poop bags. He'd forgotten the bags. *Damn it.*

Dylan stopped. "I love the sunshine. I lived in Ohio for too damn long and dealt with crappy-ass weather. There, it's only sunny for like thirty days out of the year. Sunshine is good."

"It's nice to be out of the building for a while." Zayn allowed Nugent to set the pace. He followed along behind happily. "So what did you need to speak to me about?"

"Kris." Dylan kept up beside Zayn. "Is he still trying to go straight and do mainstream stuff?"

"Yes."

"Good. I want him to read for the male lead in my family drama, *The Place We Forgot*." Dylan slipped his phone from his pocket. "I've got time next week, if he's interested. I'd like him to read for the part Eli wanted too. It's a day's work, but it's work. Think he'd want to give it a shot…er, both of them a shot?"

"I'm sure he will be. How'd you find out about him?"

"Well, partially because of you." Dylan stopped and halted Zayn. "You wouldn't get this excited about someone if they didn't have talent. I know you. The wild cards that no one thinks can do the part are exactly what we need. You have that gift of reading people. If you weren't excited about Kris, I wouldn't have even considered him. That, and I saw his auditions video from the Rock auditions. He's good. If he can make me believe he's Rock, then he can do Kennedy. Besides, I'd rather give him the shot and go with someone who can do the part than someone who is a name. Names might sell the film, but they might also tank it."

"True." Zayn nodded. He'd seen plenty of bigger-named actors kill films at the box office because they just didn't have the right spark. The name didn't sell the picture at all. "I'll let him know. He's working with Paul Holder on his latest horror film, but I'm sure he'll want to know about this."

"Either have him give me a call or you do it, whatever, but yes. Connect with me." Dylan rolled his shoulders and stretched. "I love when the actors I want are interested in working with me. That makes the whole process a little easier."

"I understand." Zayn continued to walk the dog through the park. His spirits boosted. People were interested in working with Kris. He couldn't have been happier. "Kris' ship is coming in, Nuge." He petted the dog, then headed back to the studio building.

For the next few hours, Zayn listened to more auditions. He selected the actors for the secondary and smaller parts for the film. Unlike most days, the auditions went smoother than he'd expected and the group agreed with his choices.

Once the auditions concluded for the day, Zayn hurried out to his car. He rolled the windows down, then helped the dog into the passenger seat. He rounded the hood and slid behind the wheel. Within seconds, he dialed Kris' number and waited for the call to connect. He couldn't believe Kris' luck. Even if Kris didn't end up getting the part in Dylan's film, he was getting noticed.

The call went straight to voicemail, so Zayn left a message.

"It's Zayn. I've got the best news. I need you to call me back, but Dylan Gaughn wants you to read for a tiny part in his ensemble film called *Fourth of July*. He's also considering you for a lead part in a family drama. You're tailor-made for this role. Call me back and I'll get you the information. I'm driving home, so if I don't answer right away, that's why. Congratulations, hunk."

He hung up the phone and left it in the center console as he drove across town to Kris' place. Instead of going straight to the condo, he stopped by his apartment to grab some fresh clothes and other essentials. He led Nugent up to the fourth floor and allowed the dog to run through the apartment as he gathered his things. When he went back downstairs, bag in one hand and Nugent's leash in the other, he noticed he'd left his phone in the car. *Damn it.*

Zayn plunked the bag in the car's trunk, then helped the dog back into the vehicle. He picked up his phone and sat behind the wheel of the car. The icon for a missed call flashed. He dialed Kris' number and tried to tamp down his excitement.

"Hi," Zayn said, once the call connected. "Did you get my message?"

"I did," Kris said, his voice flat.

Zayn frowned. He rolled the windows down in the vehicle and petted the dog. Kris' tone wasn't right. He sounded depressed. "What's wrong? You're not your chipper self. You should be excited."

"Oh, sure. Yeah. Whatever."

"Hold up. What's the matter?" Zayn wanted to run straight to his boyfriend. "Talk to me."

"I'm on a mountain and even I know what's going on," Kris snapped. "Come on."

"Either you're playing with me and really excited or something really bad happened. I've been in auditions all day. Care to talk to me and explain?" *Or let me in on the joke and be happy about the chance in Dylan's movie.*

"Why don't you talk to the person who posted my audition tape on the Internet? That person—who I believe you know—freaking posted a reel featuring bits from my porn movies. Paul is pissed. Like, blind rage pissed. He doesn't want much to do with me. The only thing saving my ass right now is that it's too expensive to replace me with only a day's worth of shooting left. So, yeah, I'm having a shitty ass day."

"Who would've done that?" Zayn pulled into the parking lot of a grocery store and stopped the car. "Why?"

"Does the name Eli ring a bell?"

His blood chilled. *Oh God.* He'd expected his ex to stoop to the lowest level, but to embarrass Kris? That was bad, even for Eli. Fuck. He had to fix this and fast. Kris didn't deserve to be embarrassed. He had nothing to be ashamed of—not even his porn career. Other actors started in the adult industry and without much fanfare. Eli wasn't going to get away with embarrassing his lover.

Zayn sighed. "Do you trust me?"

Chapter Eight

"I do," Kris said. "I trust you, but I don't know that I'm enough of an actor for this crap not to matter. Things have been going too well." He forked his fingers into his hair. So many things had gone right, but so many more hadn't. Negative thoughts bombarded him. He'd been crazy to think he could truly follow his passion and become a mainstream actor. People didn't make the jump from one industry to the other. James Long, Hogan Iron and Max Length…the porn names were ridiculous, but they'd been too much for his friends, James McNoon, John Hogan and Mark Merriman to overcome. Unless they were nude and thrusting into a hole, they didn't matter. He didn't want to be another one of the disaster cases, but the way things were going he didn't have much choice.

"Don't you dare get down on yourself," Zayn replied. "I'm not letting you sink. No way. Give me two hours."

"I've got plenty of time." Kris leaned against the outer wall of his trailer and watched his costar argue with Paul. He wasn't helpless, but damn it, he hadn't wanted to see the shunning coming. If he'd been in a better mood, he'd have laughed at the fight brewing between Paul and his girlfriend. The role he'd given her wasn't great and didn't showcase her acting ability at all. No wonder she'd threatened to walk off the film.

Paul stalked across the clearing and glared at Kris. "I don't want to see you right now. I'm going to be a fucking joke." He gnashed his teeth. "Fuck. I told Zayn this wouldn't matter... I lied."

"I didn't set out to screw you over," Kris snapped. "If you think I enjoy having my private parts splattered all over the Internet and being labeled a fraud for trying to pass myself off as an actor when I'm not, then you're sorely mistaken."

"That's not my problem." Paul pinched the bridge of his nose. "Where I'm fucked is that my film won't get recognition as a viable film. People will either want to see it because they want to see the freak who did porn or they'll stay away from it because of your last job. It's like I can't be trusted to bring in the right people for the film."

"Have I let you down? Have I forgotten my lines or shown up late? I screwed up once before we started filming, but I learned my lesson. You even said I've made you proud because you felt I had captured my role and made you feel like you were watching the character, not me." Kris gritted his teeth. *Damn it.*

Paul shook his head. "That's not the case any longer. I've got to combat the bad press."

"Wait, wasn't it you that said bad press was press and you were going to run with it?" Kris asked. "What exactly do you want?"

"I want to get some good press for this damn movie."

"Then let's finish it and put it out for the public to decide." Kris folded his arms. "Shunning me and having a fit won't do anyone any good. So you dump the film. Guess what happens? People find out about it and want to see it. You make a big deal about not wanting to show the thing and it'll get shown. Might not get the great press you want, but people will be nosy and want to see it. Sounds like your horror flick ends up winning."

Paul continued to glare at Kris, but didn't answer.

"I'm not sorry I did porn. I had to eat and it was my way to do that. But right now, I'm doing the job I've been given and I'm doing it the best I can," Kris snapped. "Since you don't want to see me, I'm going into my trailer. I'm under contract until tomorrow, correct? Fine. I'll have my shit out by the morning." He turned on his heel and headed into his trailer. Anger spiraled through his veins. He wanted to rip something apart. Instead, he unleashed his fury on the punching bag in his trailer. Sweat rolled off him as he smashed his knuckles into the bag. What the hell had he ever done to deserve being raked over the coals? He hadn't hurt anyone or done anything illegal, but to hear Paul and the media talk, he was one step away from the most horrible man on earth.

He collapsed on his bed and closed his eyes. His brain hurt and his hands ached. He could still see the mash-up video in his mind. Bits and pieces of his actual audition tape spliced with clips from his X-rated movies. Jesus.

Kris picked up his phone and flipped through the images. He'd done so many things since he'd come to the woods for the shoot. Running and screaming to fake being scared to death, being caked with mud and makeup in order to give the appearance of being beaten...hell, the scene in the barn where he looked like he'd had his arm ripped off didn't take much acting, but the experience had been fun. He'd been honest-to-

God scared that the guy playing the villain really would hurt him.

He tossed the phone onto the bed, then sat up. Why was he feeling sorry for himself when he could be getting his stuff around? He debated calling Dylan, but by this point, if Dylan was still interested, he'd be surprised. Zayn had said to give him two hours. What good would that do? He wasn't sure.

Kris gathered his dirty clothes from the basket and tucked them into a duffle bag. He placed his toiletries into another bag. When he'd arrived, he'd thought he'd brought too much stuff. Now packing, he realized he'd hardly brought anything at all.

"That is bullshit."

Kris tipped his head. He knew that voice. A dog barked, grabbing his attention. He knew that bark too. *Nugent? Zayn?* He hurried to the window. Sure enough, his boyfriend and Nugent stood arguing with Paul. Nugent barked as much as Zayn appeared to be shouting. Some of the argument filtered to Kris, but not much he could understand.

Kris exited the trailer and approached the group. Nugent noticed him first and broke free from Zayn. He bounded up to Kris, practically knocking Kris over.

"Hey, bud. I'm happy to see you too." He laughed, despite his frustration over the underlying situation. "You must've missed me."

"Kris." Zayn walked away from Paul. "I was hoping you hadn't left."

"I'm contracted to be here until tomorrow." Kris sat on the ground and hugged his dog. "I see Nugent tagged along."

"He's good company." Zayn folded his arms. "He missed you."

"I hope so," Kris said.

"So." Zayn's gaze switched between Kris and Paul. "We've got a problem."

"I don't need you to jump in for me." Kris stood. He kept one hand on the top of Nugent's head. "I've handled this. I'm heading out tomorrow."

"No." Zayn shook his head. "That's not how this works." He turned his attention to Paul. "What the hell? You know better than this."

"How do I know he didn't fucking upload the damn video? Huh? For all I know, he put that video online so he could get more hits on his site or something." Paul stood toe-to-toe with Zayn. "Your money and daddy can't fix that."

"There isn't anything to fix. Kris didn't have anything to do with the video. I *know* he didn't. He's been here with shitty Wi-Fi," Zayn snapped. "The person who did it has an agenda."

"God. What have you gotten me into?" Paul growled. "That shit you dated did this, didn't he? Didn't get what he wanted...again, right? I told you not to take that dick in your ass."

"I was wrong." Zayn winced. He glanced back at Kris. "I can explain."

"No need." Kris shrugged. He'd had plenty of bad relationships, but none that came back to haunt him quite like Zayn's. Still, he wasn't in any position to pass judgment.

"Just—let him finish. This will blow over. Okay?" Zayn pleaded. "This is my fault. Don't fuck him over because of my mistake."

"Fine." Paul pointed at Kris. "We do those hand shots and the voice-overs when we get back to the studio." He hesitated and sighed. "I'm sorry, Kris. Really. You were right. Your work has been good." He shook his head as he walked away.

"That's massive. Paul doesn't apologize to anyone." Zayn's shoulders sagged. "I'm sorry too. Eli...was a mistake. I've got to sort this out."

"Fine. Do what you need to." Kris stroked the dog's head. "Leave Nuge."

"You're kicking me out?" Zayn's eyes widened.

"You said you had to sort this situation out. I'm letting you go. I have work and you don't need my dog tagging along. We'll...regroup when I come home tomorrow." Kris bit back a groan. "Sound like a plan?"

"Not really, but I can't argue with you." Zayn stood in front of Kris for another moment, then walked away.

Kris massaged his temple, then patted his hip. "Come on, Nuge. Let's go into the trailer. I'll let you get used to the place, then get this filming done. I'm ready to go home."

The dog barked and climbed onto the bed. He curled up and snuggled in the bedding as if he'd lived in the trailer all his life.

"At least you're happy." Kris headed back out to the set and waited for Paul. He filmed the hand shots, holding the book and the map on the table, then holding a torch and a crumpled- piece of paper. The shots took a little more than an hour to complete.

When they were done, Paul stopped Kris. "Now we've both had our meltdowns. I'm sorry about jumping on you. It wasn't cool. I should've checked out the link better and verified the information." He offered his hand. "You've been a good scout. Your work is good. I hope you consider working with me again. I'd be glad to have you."

"I'll think about it." Kris shook hands with the director. "I'm not in breach if I go home, am I? I'd like to sleep in my own bed tonight."

"Go home. You deserve the break. I'll call you and set up a time for the voice-overs. No sweat." Paul smiled. "Enjoy."

"I will." Kris rushed back to the trailer. He gathered up the rest of his stuff, then carried his things to the car. He returned for the dog, then double-checked the trailer. He searched every drawer and bin, then yanked the blanket off the bed. He tucked the pillows and the blanket into the trunk of his car. Another once-over and then he headed back to the vehicle.

"We're going home, Nuge." He patted the dog's head. "My bed. My things. Silence." He smiled, despite the depression settling in his mind. He was going home. The first fifty miles flew by in no time. He opened the window, allowing the breeze into the vehicle. The chilly air stung his cheeks, but kept him sharp.

He turned onto the main freeway, then sped toward his part of the city. The bright lights weren't as exciting now. Because of the past? Or because of the things he'd learned? He wasn't sure.

Kris zipped down the side street to his development. When he reached the gate, he slipped his card into the reader, then made his way to his condo. The lights illuminated the street, but nothing was quite as good as pulling into his own driveway. He parked the car in the garage, then left his bags in the trunk. He'd get those tomorrow.

With Nugent leading the way, he headed inside. He switched on the lights.

"The place is cleaner than when I left," Kris murmured. The smell of Zayn's cologne lingered in the air. He'd be lying if he said he didn't miss Zayn. He sighed. He should've known he'd want his boyfriend there. Zayn had become a part of him.

"Come on, Nuge. Let's crash. I've got crap to do in the morning—like look for a real job." His ego deflated a bit. Desire was great, but it didn't pay the bills. He'd earned an apology from Paul, but the damage had been done. He locked the back door, then strode into the bedroom and collapsed on the bed. Something clunked against his head.

He flipped on the light, then grasped the object. A book. Kris frowned. What the hell? He turned the book over in his hands. *The Complete Works of Shakespeare*. He caressed the gold lettering.

The only person who knew about his love of Shakespeare was Zayn. He opened the book to the first page.

You never know what can happen when you open your heart and try.

Although part of him wanted to be far away from Zayn, the rest of him appreciated the sentiment. He grabbed his phone and dialed his…were they boyfriends? He wasn't sure. They'd argued, but hadn't broken up—had they? As much as defining relationships was considered blasé, he kind of wanted to know where they stood with each other. He dialed the number, then set the phone to the speaker setting.

"Hello?"

"Zayn?" Kris asked. He knew the voice, but wasn't sure if Zayn would even answer. "Hey."

"Hi. You sound happier."

"I am. I found your present. Thanks." He touched the leather cover on the book. "I love it."

"Present? The flowers aren't supposed to come until tomorrow. What are you talking about?" Zayn asked. "I'm confused."

"You didn't leave a book on my bed?"

"Book? No."

Kris' stomach churned. He dropped the book. "You're serious. A book of Shakespeare—it wasn't you?"

"Although that sounds like something I'd give you, I didn't."

Kris glanced around the room. Nothing else appeared to be out of place. Still, he didn't feel right. Something was wrong. "You did or didn't clean up?"

"I cleaned, but that's because Nugent and I left the place a mess."

"Shit." Kris rubbed his arms. He didn't have anything of real value in the condo other than the dog. Most of his stuff was nice, but not extravagant. Still, he didn't like having his home violated. "Okay."

"Okay? What?"

"I'm calling the police. Something isn't right." Kris stood. He surveyed the room. Nothing else appeared to be out of place, but he couldn't shake the uneasy feeling.

"I'll be over in ten." Zayn hung up, leaving Kris in silence.

The lack of sound unnerved Kris even more. He snatched the phone from the bed, then watched Nugent. The dog initially climbed onto the blankets, then jumped off the mattress and paced the room with his nose to the ground.

"What, boy?" Kris dialed the police and continued to watch the dog. Nugent stopped at the closet and pawed at the carpet.

While he gave the nine-one-one operator his information, he kept his attention on Nugent. "Thank you," he said and hung up. Seconds later, red and blue lights flashed outside the condo.

Kris met the police at the front door a few minutes later. "I touched the book, but it's still on the bed." He pointed to the bedroom. "It's not from my boyfriend and I don't have anyone else with access to my home."

"You're sure? When did you discover the item?" the officer asked.

"About half an hour ago. I just came home from a movie shoot. I wasn't supposed to get in until tomorrow, but filming wrapped early. Anyway, I came home, parked the car and came inside. I'd planned to flop on the bed and crash, but when I did, this clunked me in the head." Kris stepped back from the cop. "My dog hasn't stopped sniffing the closet. Search it. I have nothing to hide."

"Do you have tags for the dog? He's considered a vicious breed."

"I do have the tags, but I disagree about the vicious part." Kris produced the proper identification and tags. "I need to renew them next month, but he's legal right now."

"Good." The officer investigated the outside of the closet, then opened the door. A box sat in the middle of the clothing. "Excuse me, sir, I need you to step out of the room."

Kris nodded and grabbed Nugent's collar. He led the dog into the living room. Another officer pointed to the front yard. "Wait outside."

He sighed and did as told. Kris vacated his home. Brakes screeched behind him. When he turned around, Zayn barreled up the walkway.

"Any news?" He gathered Kris in a hug.

"Nothing." Kris rested his head on Zayn's shoulder. "I'm worn out."

"I know. The shoot took a lot out of you, then the thing with Paul..." Zayn stroked Kris' hair. "I'm not going to leave you alone."

"Excuse me." One of the officers approached Kris. "Are you in the habit of keeping raw meat in your closet?"

"Raw meat?" Kris cringed. "I haven't been home for the last two and a half weeks."

"Who has had access to your home?" he asked.

"I have." Zayn stood tall. "I've been house and dog sitting."

"Did you leave meat in the closet?" The officer snorted. "Maybe a present for the dog?"

"No." Zayn shook his head. "His treats were in the fridge."

"Where have you been for the last twenty-four hours? You're supposed to be house-sitting. If he's come home early, then you should be here." The officer folded his arms.

"I went to work at National Colors Studio, doing auditions for the latest film by Dylan Gaughn. After a discussion with Mr. Gaughn in the courtyard of the studio, I took Nugent with me to the shoot for Paul Holden. I met with Kris, argued and left the dog there. I've been at my apartment since, answering emails and fielding phone calls about another film." Zayn matched the officer's stance. "You can check with the studio."

"What did you argue about?"

"My ex had something done to Kris. Someone I used to be involved with posted a video of Kris. It wasn't tasteful or truthful." Zayn rubbed his face with both hands. "It's complicated, but basically he's trying to get out of porn and into mainstream movies. My ex—Eli Marsters—can't take no for an answer."

"I see." The officer scribbled something onto a pad of paper. He strolled away from Kris and Zayn.

"I'm sorry." Zayn rubbed Kris' back. "I had no idea."

"You still don't. For all we know, Eli wasn't behind this," Kris snapped.

"And for all we know, he was." Zayn sighed. He stepped in front of Kris. "My batshit crazy ex doesn't have the power here. You do. Your career isn't over. So a video was posted? Own it. Yes, you did that stuff and yes, you did other stuff, but it's all your body of work."

"It's my ass sticking out," Kris growled. No need to bring attention to them, but he doubted the cops were missing the argument.

"It's a very nice ass too." Zayn stepped closer to Kris. "You can't run from your past. God knows I've tried. It's not possible. So what's the next best thing? You own it. Call Dylan tomorrow and set up that audition. You nail it just like you did the one for Paul and the first one for me. You're bigger than this stupid incident with the video."

"My home was invaded." Kris pointed to the condo. "Someone left raw meat in my closet."

Zayn's shoulders sagged.

"I feel violated all over again." Kris marched over to the curb and sat on the concrete. Nugent snuggled up beside him. "What am I supposed to do? My home is a crime scene."

"Come home with me." Zayn sat on the other side of him. "I've got space."

"It's not a matter of space. It's... This feels like when I was thirteen all over again. I can't change what happened. I didn't ask for this." He shook his head. The disgust, the anger and pain washed over him all over again. His stomach roiled, just as it had that night. He closed his eyes and leaned forward with his head between his knees.

Instead of saying anything, Zayn rubbed Kris' back. The rhythmic stroking comforted him, but he still bit back bile.

"Someone knew how to get to me," Kris said. "They not only invaded my space, but they fucked with my head. For all I know, there was something in that meat to kill my dog."

"The police will handle it. That's what they get paid to do." Zayn continued to rub Kris' back. "I'm not leaving you. I wish I could say I was quick enough to have gifted you with that book. It was a good idea. The meat...not so much."

Kris lifted his head. "Destroy my stuff and fuck with my head, but don't fuck with my dog. I hate when the dog gets killed off in the movies."

One of the officers, the detective who'd asked all the questions, strode up to Kris. "We're going to seal off your condo for the time being. Until all evidence is processed and we can ascertain what meat that was and what might be in it, we'd like you to remain off the premises. Do you have somewhere to stay?"

Kris glanced over at Zayn. Although they'd been arguing, he didn't trust anyone else. "I do."

"And a number where we can reach you? I'll need you to come down to the precinct tomorrow for your statement."

"My number is on the initial report. I gave it to the other officers." Kris' hand shook. "But my phone is inside, along with my keys and my wallet."

"You can use my number." Zayn rattled off his phone number to the police officer, then draped his arm around Kris.

"There will an officer guarding the condo until we've finished processing. I'll see that your personal items are brought to the station. Can you think of anyone who would want to harm you or your pet?"

"I—I never thought about it." Kris shook his head. "I did porn. Any of my directors who made money off my films or even the adult studio could be doing this as a scare tactic to get me to come back. It could be his ex-boyfriend. I've never met the guy, but anything is possible."

"Anyone else?" the officer prompted.

"No. None I can think of."

"We'll see you at the station tomorrow for the formal statement." The officer nodded once, then left Kris and Zayn alone.

"I've got you." Zayn slid his hand down to Kris' and squeezed. "We'll get through this."

Kris sighed. "Just take me…home, I guess." He felt Zayn's grasp on his hand, but barely noticed. He heard the people talking, but none of the words made sense. Everything seemed blurry. He allowed Zayn to help him onto the passenger seat. Nugent climbed on his lap, then slid to the floor. The dog whimpered until Kris petted him.

He stared out of the window as the world passed by. Why did this have to happen? He wasn't trying to change everything, just a little part of the universe. So he wanted out of porn. That didn't make him horrible. So he wanted a career in regular films. Who didn't?

Zayn pulled the car to a stop and turned off the engine. "Welcome to Chateau du Mason. It's not the high life, but it costs about that much." He trailed his fingers over Kris' cheek. "I'm not the only one in the film industry who lives here. Tony Bosa lives in that building. George Lott lives two floors up from me and

Cassidy Brown has a unit over in C building. The studios all have guards to protect their investments. I happen to have the security teams by default. Something happens to them, someone will know."

"I should be flattered, but I'm not." Kris rested his head on the back of the seat. "This is a nightmare."

"Come inside with me and take a break from it. The crap isn't going away, but this will be a few hours' respite." Zayn left the car and rounded the hood. He opened the door. "Come on."

Kris allowed the dog to leave the car first, then followed. The ache behind his eyes had increased. His jaw hurt from clenching his teeth. The words in the book had imprinted themselves in his memory. Why? Why would someone want to hurt him like that?

"Stretch out on the bed with Nugent. I'll be in once I lock up." Zayn nodded to the hallway. "The only door on the right."

Kris wandered to the bedroom and collapsed on the bed. The dog jumped onto the mattress beside him and stretched out. He petted the animal and willed his heart rate to return to the normal range.

"I gave the detective my number. He called. They didn't find anything else out of the ordinary, but they're keeping the guard there through the night and are going back in the morning." Zayn patted Kris' ankle. "Sit up. I'll help you lose your shirt."

Kris did as told and allowed Zayn to remove the garment.

"I'm here when you're ready to talk." Zayn settled beside him. "I can't exactly say I know what you're going through. I've cast roles about this kind of thing — stalking and abuse — but I've never had to deal with it, myself."

Kris rested one hand on his belly and the other on the dog's back. He wasn't sure what to say, but allowed the words to flow. "Do you remember asking me about my tattoos?"

"I do." Zayn rested his palm on top of Kris'.

"I said there was a story there, but I wasn't ready to tell you. I'm ready." He sighed. "The initials on my neck are mine. I didn't want to forget who I was. After the crap that happened when I was a kid and the betrayal by my mother, I wanted to stay true to myself. It hurt like hell to get that tattoo, but it was worth the pain."

"I like it." Zayn kissed Kris' shoulder. "It's sexy."

"Thanks." Kris moved his hand from his belly to Zayn's hip. "The *Superman* 'S' is there because I wanted to be more than just the porn star. Two sides to my story. I'm not sure how well that's going, but I decided to think positive." His mind eased. Yes, the shit from the condo still bothered him, but he was safe.

"You were right to think that way. You're going to rise above this." Zayn kissed Kris' temple. "You're a good actor."

"Well, we'll find out."

"We will. Dylan was really interested. You can't obsess on this garbage with the video. Own it."

Kris chuckled. For the first time since the whole situation started, he felt lighter. The problem wasn't over, but he felt better. "I hate thinking about it that way, but you're right. I *am* that Superman. I have more than one side to my persona. I should market myself as having unique skills."

"You do." Zayn snuggled closer to him. "You're the man of many talents."

"Something like that."

"What about the horse? Why a dark horse? You think you're going to be counted out?" Zayn asked.

"That's it. Between my mother swearing I was worthless because of…you know." He still didn't want to talk about his past. He'd opened up, but once was enough. "Then there was the crap in college and now this. I'm tired of being counted out, but I kind of like the dark horse status."

"It suits you."

Kris closed his eyes and settled. "What about you? Ever wanted a tattoo?"

"Nah. I couldn't decide what I wanted, so I never went through with it. Eli wanted me to have his name inked onto my ass. I declined."

"Good thing."

"You bet it is. I always sort of knew he wasn't going to be a forever guy, but I wanted to be in a relationship so much I overlooked a lot and shortchanged myself. He never was right for me." Zayn tangled his legs with Kris'. "I've always known what I want when it comes to movies, but not in my love life." He propped himself up on his elbow and tipped Kris' chin, catching Kris' gaze. "I can't change what Eli did with that video, and yeah, I had it traced. Eli manipulated it. I don't know why he would've done that, but don't let it bother you. I know actors and you've got what it takes. I'm serious."

"I'll try. All I've ever wanted to do was act." Kris kicked out of his shoes. "Movies are your thing?"

"They are. When I was a kid, I wanted to make my own films. I drove my parents crazy with my different cameras. I'd film pretty much everything." He laughed. "My father made so many movies. He was the reason I got into films. I wanted to be like him."

"What's your favorite part?" Kris yawned. Sleep filled his brain. He loved talking to Zayn. The conversation kept his mind off the other things and helped him to learn more about his boyfriend.

"The ladies of the silver screen. I loved how they seemed larger than life and so beautiful. I wasn't attracted to them, but I wanted to watch them. When I got older, I wanted to film them, but I've got no mind for framing. I can see the character and how I want the character portrayed, but sorting out how they'll appear in the scene and how to set up the scene…that's beyond my capabilities."

"You're good at your job—and I am getting sleepy." Kris nuzzled Zayn's neck. "Part of me wants to fuck you and the rest of me wants to say to hell with this night and sleep."

"We can screw all we want in the morning. I'm not going anywhere." Zayn grabbed a blanket and draped it across their bodies. "I promise."

"Works for me," Kris said and sighed. With his man on one side and the dog on the other, his mind eased. Things weren't great, but for now, he'd accept what was happening. "I'm sorry I got upset."

"I'm sorry too. I get wrapped up in what I want and doing things the way I see fit. It's cost me relationships before." Zayn draped his arm across Kris' chest. "I can't say we're going to go the distance, but if you're willing to work, so am I. You're the best thing that's happened to me in a long time…boyfriend."

Kris chuckled and nodded. "Okay." If he said anything else, he couldn't remember. His mind went blank and he succumbed to sleep. All the things that had happened that day could be dealt with tomorrow. He needed something honest and safe and he found both in Zayn's arms. His boyfriend was right—there wasn't a guarantee they'd end up together for good, but he liked their odds.

Chapter Nine

Zayn woke with a start and stared at the person beside him. Or rather, the individuals beside him. He rarely shared his bed and seeing both Kris and Nugent on the mattress surprised then comforted him. They were there. He watched Kris sleep. The man was handsome awake, but there was a certain ethereal quality to him when he slept. Almost angelic, but devilish at the same time.

Zayn scooted out of bed, careful not to wake his boyfriend or the dog. He'd always been an early riser and being in his own home, he'd adjusted back to his regular schedule. He strode into the kitchen to start the coffee. Four scoops of grounds into the machine along with enough water for ten cups of the brew would be enough to get him started. Once he scrolled through his email and the latest news on his tablet, he'd be ready to tackle the day.

He tapped the email icon on the tablet. The usual messages about auditions, follow-ups with directors and queries from actors filled his email, but one grabbed his attention. He recognized the address immediately.

Eli.

Open it and chance a virus? The jerk had already created a video mash-up of Kris' work. Was he capable of doing something more sinister? Probably. Zayn refused to chance the integrity of his tablet.

He picked up his phone. The icon for missed calls flashed. He didn't remember hearing the device ring. He scrolled through the screens to the correct page.

"Fifteen missed calls?" he blurted. He glanced around the room. Shit. He hadn't meant to say that out loud. None of the numbers looked familiar, so he retrieved the card the detective had given him. Still, none of the digits matched up.

The scent of brewing coffee wafted through the air. He breathed in the inviting smell and sighed. Since he didn't know the person or persons who'd called him, he'd simply leave the info on the phone. When he talked to the detective later, he'd bring up the issue.

"I thought we were going to fuck this morning." Kris wandered into the kitchen. "That smells awesome."

"I like a tall, dark one before I start my day." Zayn wrapped his arms around Kris.

"Coffee or me?"

"Both. But you taste a whole lot better." He kissed Kris on the lips and groaned. He loved the way Kris tasted and how he curled into Zayn.

"Then come back to bed. The coffee can wait." Kris tugged Zayn from the kitchen. "I don't want the day to start."

"Why?"

"Then the rest of the world has crashed our party. I'm not ready for this to end." Kris toppled backward onto the bed and pulled Zayn on top of him.

"Who says it has to end?" Zayn straddled Kris' hips. He draped his arms around Kris' shoulders and locked lips with his boyfriend. He shivered and cuddled into Kris' arms.

"Want to fuck you." Kris yanked Zayn's shirt up over his head and tossed the garment out of sight. "You are..." He pinched Zayn's pierced nipple. "Hot."

Zayn rolled his hips, rubbing the bulge in his pants against the one in Kris' pants. He'd always been a more submissive lover. When Kris nudged Zayn off his lap and took control, Zayn's heart raced. *Hell yeah.*

Kris pushed him onto the bed. He kissed a path of fire along Zayn's chest, taking extra time on Zayn's nipple. He bit the tender flesh, then flicked Zayn's chest. Pain shot through his body and centered in his groin. He groaned.

"Like that?" Kris glanced up into Zayn's eyes while he unbuttoned Zayn's pants. He swirled his tongue around Zayn's belly button. The light flicker intoxicated Zayn.

Zayn dug his fingers into the bedding and whimpered. "I need more."

"You'll get more." Kris tugged Zayn's pants to the floor. His eyes lit up. "Damn. You never cease to amaze me."

"How?" Zayn propped himself up on his elbows and watched Kris. "I'm not that exciting." But being with Kris was exhilarating.

"You are." Kris wrapped his fingers around Zayn's dick and stroked. He flicked his tongue across the blunt head of Zayn's dick. "You taste good too." He plunged his mouth down on Zayn's cock, swallowing him to the root.

Zayn tensed. He forked his fingers into Kris' hair. He didn't have to set the pace. Kris managed a great speed on his own. He bobbed his head, engulfing Zayn's dick and then pulling out to the tip.

"Holy shit." Zayn gritted his teeth. His skin prickled with perspiration. He propped his feet on the frame of the bed. His balls tingled. "Suck my balls."

"Pushy." Kris nibbled along Zayn's shaft. He slid one hand under Zayn's testicles. He massaged Zayn and hummed.

"Fuck." Zayn yanked on Kris' hair. "Love that."

Kris stroked him and sucked one of Zayn's balls into his mouth. The new sensations rocked Zayn's body. His thoughts blurred and he couldn't breathe. Words escaped him. When Kris grasped Zayn's legs, then pinned Zayn's knees to his chest, Zayn whimpered. He loved being folded up like a pretzel — especially if he was about to get fucked. He held on to his ankles.

"Take me," Zayn murmured. "My ass is yours."

"Not yet." Kris nibbled on Zayn's balls, then bobbed his head and fucked Zayn's cock with his mouth. When he swallowed Zayn to the back of his throat, he caressed the head of Zayn's dick.

"That feels like heaven." Zayn tipped his head back and closed his eyes. Heat centered in his belly. He writhed, pushing his dick into Kris' mouth and rolling his hips. His resistance held by a thread.

Kris hummed again, but this time he pressed the tip of one of his fingers against Zayn's asshole.

"Fuck," Zayn said again and opened his eyes. He pulled on Kris' hair. "My God."

"Like that?" Kris tapped Zayn's hole. "I'm taking this."

"Yeah," Zayn said and nodded. "Please?"

Kris stood. He whipped his shirt up over his head, then shoved his pants to the floor.

"No underwear?" Zayn blurted. "I assumed, but...seeing is very good."

"Just good?" Kris rolled his shoulders, flexing his muscles. The act turned Zayn on even more. Kris stroked his own dick a couple of times. "We need rubbers and lube."

"In the wooden box there." Zayn pointed to the nightstand. "I've got lots."

"Good." Kris smiled, his grin wolfish. He opened the lid on the box and withdrew both the bottle of lube and a rubber. "Want me?"

"I do." Zayn grabbed his ass and pulled his cheeks apart. "Please?"

"All in good time." Kris sheathed himself, then dribbled the clear liquid over his cock. He dumped another dollop of lube on his fingers. He leaned between Zayn's legs and stuffed his finger into Zayn's ass.

Zayn bore down on Kris and accepted the invasion into his body. He shivered again. His legs trembled. The heat in his veins increased. "I'm not going to last."

"Then I won't make you wait." Kris withdrew his finger, then lined up his dick with Zayn's asshole. "Breathe."

"I'm trying." The excitement got the better of Zayn. He let go of his legs and propped his ankles on Kris' shoulders. The orgasm careened through him. "I can't hold back."

"I haven't started." Kris pushed himself balls deep into Zayn. He grasped Zayn's hips and built up a steady rhythm. In and out, he claimed his lover's ass.

"You make me come apart." Zayn met Kris thrust for thrust. He squeezed down on Kris, loving the way he felt every ripple and vein in his boyfriend's erection. The tangy scent of sweat hung in the air and perspiration glistened on Kris' chest. His eyes widened and he parted his lips. The taste of Kris' kiss lingered in Zayn's mind.

"Fucking hell." Kris dug his fingers into Zayn's skin. He closed his eyes and grunted. "Sweet Jesus." He shuddered and his dick throbbed. "Come for me."

Zayn stroked himself. He groaned and yanked on his cock. "I'm right there."

"Zayn." Kris tensed. He leaned over Zayn and crushed his mouth onto Zayn's. He swallowed Zayn's moans. When he broke for air, Kris grunted. His erection twitched deep in Zayn's ass.

Zayn clutched Kris' shoulders. "Holy hell." His restraint shattered. Cum shot across his belly and another rope splattered onto Kris' stomach. The room whirled and Zayn fought to keep his eyes open. He hadn't felt so wrung out in a long time.

"That's good." Kris eased himself out of Zayn's hole.

Zayn closed his eyes and fought for air. He didn't see Kris move, but he heard the snap of a condom being removed. The bed sagged, then Kris draped his arm across Zayn's belly.

"You've got a body made for porn, but I'm glad it's all mine." Kris nipped Zayn's shoulder.

Once Zayn processed Kris' words, a question came to mind. "This wasn't like your shoot." He turned his head to look at Kris.

"I'm with someone I want to be with. I didn't have to act. You're hot and get me right on the edge." Kris grinned. "Sexy man." He frowned. "Wait. What is that noise?" He scrubbed both hands over his face. "Your phone or mine? I knew someone would have to call right now."

"Probably mine." Zayn left the bed long enough to retrieve his phone. He recognized the number. "It's Paul."

"Shit," Kris muttered.

"Don't get down on yourself. You don't know why he's calling." Zayn pressed the button to answer the call. "Hello?"

"Zayn, I'm glad I caught you. Where's your boy?" Paul asked. He puffed, as if he were out of breath.

"Here with me. Why?" He sat on the bed and leaned back against Kris. "Now what's wrong? Are you trying to call and jog at the same time again? You know it's not a good idea."

"I'm multitasking. Shut up," Paul snapped, but without venom in his voice. "I finished editing. Went better than I expected. Your boy isn't a giggler, so we didn't have tons of outtakes. Anyway, the reason I'm calling is because of the movie," he said. "You're never going to believe this, but I presented the rough cut of the film to people at the studio. I didn't name my cast, since it was the rough cut, but the heads can't get enough of Kris."

"No shitting?" Zayn patted Kris' leg, then snapped his fingers. He turned to face his boyfriend and mouthed, 'good news'. Kris rolled his eyes, then flopped back onto the pillow.

"Would I lie about a movie? Especially one that's going to make me money? No. I'm serious."

"Wow—although I'm not surprised. He's got something, you know?" Zayn massaged Kris' biceps. Finally, someone else was seeing the desire deep within Kris. The world would understand that this porn king really had the stuff to cross over to mainstream films. Hell, he *belonged* in mainstream movies.

"I do now. Dylan called me. He's even seen the film. He should be getting in touch with you soon. If Kris doesn't nab that ensemble film, I'll eat my hat," Paul said. "Think he'd be willing to overlook my jackass-ness and work with me again? I've got a gritty LGBT title that might be up his alley. I'll email you the script. See what you think and get his opinion. I trust you. I never thought I'd say that again, but yeah. I do."

Zayn's heart pounded. He knew the mash-up video wouldn't be the death knell for Kris. He couldn't wait to share the good news. "I'll see what I can make happen. No guarantees."

"Understood. Thanks." Paul clicked off the line.

Zayn dropped the device onto his lap, then patted Kris' belly. "You're never going to believe this. Paul showed the rough cut to the studio people. I guess he got backing from Zephyr Studios. Whatever works, but honestly, it's a great thing. They saw you. The studio heads don't know who you are and judged you based on your work."

"Fuck." The color drained from Kris' face. "And?"

"They loved it." Zayn applauded. He jumped to his feet and whooped. "They want more."

"But they don't know my name." Kris shook his head. "This can't end well."

"Stop. This can end well. They can't judge you on anything but that." Zayn crawled on top of Kris again. "When we're considering someone for a role, the audition is the only thing we consider — well, that and your work ethic and personality, but you've nailed both of those too."

"I don't see how you can be so positive."

"Because I believe in you." Zayn bounced on Kris' lap. "There is so much more to you than your past — all of your past. You're a wonderful actor and you're starting to get noticed for that work." His phone buzzed in his hand. He read the ID screen. "Ha! This is Dylan." He swiped the screen to answer. "Hello."

"Aren't you chipper? You'd think someone called to ask for your boyfriend to audition for a movie," Dylan said. "You haven't called me back concerning the offer I gave you."

"We've had a few snags in the last couple of days. It's a long story and I'll explain it later." Zayn climbed off Kris and paced the length of his bedroom. "What can I do for you?"

"It's not so much what you can do, but what I need from Kris. Is he willing to do the audition?" Dylan asked.

"How about you speak to him." Zayn handed the phone over to Kris. "It's for you and it's a good thing."

Kris sat up. He took the phone, then narrowed his eyes at Zayn. He'd get over the irritation soon enough. Once he found out why Dylan had called, he'd be thrilled. Zayn listened to Kris' end of the conversation.

"You really want me?" Kris clutched the phone. "I — I hadn't expected it. After the video...well, no, I didn't create it. It's all my work, yeah." His eyes widened. "I need to take care of some things this morning, but yes, I can meet with you. Thank you." He kept the phone glued to his ear for another few moments, then handed the device back to Zayn. His lips parted, but no sound came out. He stared at Zayn.

Zayn checked the phone screen. Dylan was still there. "Hey. So, I'm assuming things went the way you wanted?" He bottled his excitement — for now. Things were starting to turn around for Kris. He refused to let Kris blow the chance. Sure, they'd been through a whole lot of shit in the last few hours, but he wasn't giving up on Kris.

"He's in shock, I'd guess," Dylan said. "Just have him to Zephyr at three. If there's a problem—whatever needs taken care of—let me know. Text me or whatever. I really want to get moving on this project."

"You've got it. Later." Zayn hung up then grinned at Kris. "So?" He wanted to jump up and down. Scream. Whoop and holler. "What's going through that sexy head of yours?" He shouldn't get so worked up, but he believed in Kris.

"I've got another audition. I can't believe it." Kris laced his fingers together on top of his head. "Dylan wasn't fazed by the video. He viewed it, but considered it more as a showcase, rather than something bad. I don't know how you knew, but you were right." He smiled. "He saw my dick and didn't... He saw past it. How do you do that? Look past someone's crap and keep giving them a chance."

"I've been around this block a few times." Zayn sat in front of Kris. "You're meant for more than taking your clothes off and having sex." Now Kris was starting to see what everyone else saw—he had the potential to be a huge star.

"You liked it when we took our clothes off and had sex." Kris grinned wider. His shoulders slumped and he exhaled, but the sparkle remained in his eyes. "I might be able to turn my passion into a decent paycheck."

"I'm sure you can." Without a doubt. Kris could do anything he wanted to and Zayn would back him up.

"First, we have to talk to the police. Find out what they know and see if I can get back into my condo. I don't like not having access to my stuff." Kris left the bed and strolled around the room, buck-ass nude. His muscles flexed with each step. "I need to talk to him, shower, shave and prep for this role—whatever it is.

I'm not even sure what he wants me for." He rested his hands on his lower back, accentuating the gentle curve of his ass.

Zayn couldn't tear his gaze from his boyfriend. The man moved with fluid grace. Nude or clothed, he personified sexiness.

"You do know you're fine as hell." Zayn stopped Kris mid-stride and caged him between his legs. "I can't think straight with you wandering around naked."

"It's a gift." Kris shrugged. His cock bounced against Zayn's thigh. "I'm used to being naked. That's easy. What's not easy is prepping for this role. I don't know what to expect."

"It's probably a dry reading. He'll give you a couple pages and expect you to do something with it right then and there. It's standard for some studios. They know you can interpret if you've been given time to prepare, but if you're working with someone who does improvisation, then they want to be sure you can work with it." God, he wanted to jump Kris' bones and show him just how much he'd fallen for the ex-porn star.

"Oh." Kris frowned. He grasped Zayn's shoulders and massaged the muscle. "They haven't seen a porn set. There's a script, but no one sticks to it. That would require the players to actually know how to act, how to memorize lines and how to deliver said lines while trying to fuck someone."

He'd seen Kris at work on the porn set. He wasn't sure about the script issue, but Kris seemed so at-home and confident. He'd be able to handle a regular shoot with improv as well as any actor. "Then you should be fine. Come on. We'll go to the station and get that over with."

"First, I need to take Nugent for a walk. He's been good, but I'm sure he'll have to go." Kris picked up his shirt, then yanked the denim down past his head. His hair stuck out in wild tangles, but the just-out-of-bed look worked for him. "Ready?"

"Sure, but you need to get dressed in more than just a shirt. The security around here is great, but the paparazzi still hangs out beyond the gate. They'd certainly pay attention if you're out and about flashing your dick." Zayn tossed a pair of boxer shorts at Kris. "You can borrow those."

"You're saying I have to wear pants?" Kris grinned. "Paparazzi. The only press I used to deal with was people wanting to break into the sets so they could have sex with us." He donned the boxer shorts, then stepped into his rumpled pants. "You'd be surprised how many women will crash a set to sleep with Hogan Iron and Max Length. Corny-ass names, but they got the action."

Zayn crossed the room to where Kris stood and wrapped his arms around his man. He breathed in Kris' scent and nuzzled the side of Kris' neck. "They aren't you. I'm not interested."

Kris groaned. He slid his hands into Zayn's back pockets. "You're one of the very few. I was popular because I did my job, didn't do drugs or smoke, knew my lines and wasn't fucked up with an STD."

"Sounds like your competition wasn't much...er...competition." Zayn leaned back in Kris' embrace. "Seriously. You sound almost impossibly good. Didn't you have any vices?"

"I like a good red wine in the evenings and I used to sleep around. I'm not good or perfect. I made my mistakes." Kris rested his forehead against Zayn's. They swayed together. Despite the tone of the conversation, they had a good rapport. "The women are easy to come by. Plenty of girls want to make a name in porn. Most of them are blonde and blue-eyed.

You'd swear they stepped off the farm and stopped by the breast enhancement clinic along the way. But the guys...there are a few more requirements. The directors want guys who are hot, but you've got to be six inches, minimum. Horrible, but true. If you're small, don't call. If you're big, we've got a gig."

"That's terrible." *Odd for us to be having the conversation about how to get ahead in porn,* Zayn thought. But they'd fallen into the discussion so easily.

"It was on one guy's business cards. I never worked for him, but I remember seeing it." He put his socks, then boots on and stood. "If you're willing to go bare—meaning, no condom—you can make a killing too." He patted his hip. "Ready, Nugent?"

The dog sashayed around his legs and barked once.

"Guess that means he's good." Zayn tucked his keys into the pocket of his hoodie. "I just need my shoes and I'm good too."

"Let's go." Kris secured the leash to Nugent's collar, then wrapped the other end of the leash around his hand.

Zayn settled on Kris' other side and fell into step with him and the dog. "You said you never went bare."

"I couldn't. Too much to chance. Sure, it's sexier on screen. There's no latex in the way. But I needed to be safe." He offered his hand to Zayn. "I like knowing my partners and not being in jeopardy more than I have to be."

Zayn grinned. Why bother holding his good feeling back? He was with the guy he'd fallen for and they appeared to the rest of the world like a long-term couple. As they walked, neither of them said anything. Zayn's thoughts turned their situation. He knew what he wanted in life—he wanted to cast movies and see the actors and actresses best meant for the role portraying the characters on the screen. He embraced his love of filmmaking and setting the right people in the right roles. As for his love life, that's where he didn't know what he wanted — until now. His heart belonged to Kris. He wanted to wake up beside his boyfriend and see Kris' face the last thing before he went to bed.

"We're back at your building, but I don't feel like you're with me." Kris stopped in front of Zayn and grinned. "You in there?"

Zayn sighed. "I am. I was thinking. Sorry." He unlocked the door, then escorted Kris and Nugent upstairs. "You're going to Zephyr for the audition. I need to head there, too, so we can bring Nuge along. I've taken him with me to almost all the auditions I've been in charge of and he's been a champ. If I keep him with me, that lets you worry about the part without having worry about the dog."

"Sounds good." Once inside the apartment, Kris squeezed Zayn's hand. "Thanks."

"No problem. Nugent and I have an understanding. He's got my back. He also keeps my feet warm." Zayn chuckled. "He sleeps through the auditions. Not good for the actors, but great for me."

Kris shook his head. "That's not what I meant, but I am thankful."

"I'm lost." He wasn't sure what the hell Kris meant.

Kris let go of the leash and pinned Zayn to the wall. "I meant, thank you. Because of you, I have faith in mankind again. I know things don't always work out, but I can't lose faith. I thought I was at the lowest point when I auditioned for you and now I see it. I understand. I had to go through that crap so I could become a better actor. I always had the drive, but because I've got someone in my corner I have more faith in myself."

"You've always had what it takes to be a star. You needed the nudge to go the extra distance." Zayn kissed Kris on the lips. He savored the taste of his boyfriend on his tongue. He groaned.

"If you left me, I could still act and probably still manage to get through the auditions, but I'm glad I've got you," Kris said. "I could live without you, but I don't want to."

"I feel the same way." Zayn swatted Kris' ass. "Let's get those statements done. We'll pick up Nugent and head to the condo. Yeah?"

"Sounds great." Kris grinned. "Really great."

* * * *

An hour later, Zayn sat in one of the rooms at the police station. The sickening gray-green walls seemed to close in on him. The acrid scent of sanitizer hung in the air. He choked back a gag. He stared at the piece of paper. He'd filled out the form describing his whereabouts for the day before, but hadn't seen the detective in ten minutes. Where in the hell was the guy?

He spun the pen on the table and groaned. How many people had sat at that exact table and wondered their fate? Probably too many. But being on the other side of the situation, he understood the tremendous pressure. The actors who portrayed characters having been incarcerated or about to be incarcerated. The stress alone would kill him and he hadn't done anything wrong.

The door opened and the detective finally entered the room. "I've got a few questions before I let you go. Now, I'm not holding you, but we did have to do some checking. Your alibi was a little shaky." He plunked a folder onto the table, then sat on the metal chair. The legs scraped against the floor and grated on Zayn's nerves.

"Where were you around nine last night?" The detective clicked his pen and opened the folder.

"As I've said on this paper, I was in the middle of about five things. I called Dylan Gaughn just before nine. We talked for about ten minutes or so. Then I placed a call to Paul Holden. I got his voice mail and left him a message. While I did all that, I emailed my friend, Roy Donegan to trace a video. He sent a reply and did as I asked. At nine-thirty, once I'd heard back from Roy, I got in touch with my ex, Eli. I gave him a piece of my mind because he was the jerk who posted the audition reel of Kris Hunter. He had no right to post that video." Zayn folded his hands. He had nothing to be worried about, and yet he felt like he was the one on trial.

"You've got quite an interest in Mr. Hunter. One could assume you'd be happier if Mr. Hunter didn't cross over from porn to mainstream work because then he'd be reliant on you." The detective narrowed his eyes. "Am I wrong?"

"Very. I want him to make it big. Hell, I can see his name in lights and on gigantic posters. He's got raw talent and drive. He's meant for motion pictures." Zayn crossed his ankles. "Anything else? Asking me questions about my interest in Kris isn't getting this case solved."

"You're blunt, aren't you?" The detective flipped through the pages in the folder. "According to Mr. Hunter, you fought earlier in the day. Care to tell me what about?"

"We got into a disagreement over the video. He thought I'd mashed up his prior work with the audition tape. I hadn't, but since his director on his most recent film, Paul Holden, proceeded to fire him, he wasn't listening to me. I spoke to Paul and got things sorted out. Things with Mr. Hunter took a little longer, but we're on much better terms." Christ. He hadn't expected to hash out the details of his life for the past twenty-four hours.

"I see. We've run your phone records and Internet usage. Your story checks out."

"Oh good," Zayn snapped.

"Don't be a jerk."

"I'm not trying to be, but I've cooperated. I love Mr. Hunter. Why in the hell would I try to ruin the career I'm trying to help him build?" Zayn groaned. "It's nuts."

The detective stared at him. If Zayn had been casting the role of asshole detective, the guy would've won on attitude alone. As for looks, he fit the bill there too. The lines around the guy's eyes were etched deep. When he ran his fingers over his hair, a few more strands fell out and increased his receding hairline. He could've stood to lose at least thirty pounds too. Zayn plopped his hands into his lap.

"Congratulations. You're in love," the detective grumbled. He shook his head. "You're free to go for now, but expect more questions. I know where to find you."

"I'm available." Zayn stood, then pushed the chair in. With his head held high, he marched out of the cramped room and into the hallway. He walked down the corridor to the main lobby. Kris sat on one of the benches with his phone and keys in hand.

"Did they take blood?" Kris asked and stood. "You were in there forever."

"I know." Zayn sighed. "How long was long? It felt like forever."

"Just over an hour. I was asked about my former career, my future career, my friends, anyone who might hate my guts and Eli. I did what they wanted, filled out the paperwork and got my stuff back. They'll find out exactly what was in the hamburger, but all signs lead to poisoning. Someone wanted to kill my dog." Kris fisted his keys. "I called a locksmith too. I don't want the same locks on my condo. If I have to, I'm upping my security system as well. This isn't going to happen again."

"You're smart." Zayn grasped Kris' free hand and walked out of the precinct. "I need air." Once in the parking lot, he stretched and drank in the sunshine. "Let's get Nugent, then visit the condo so you can shower and such, then I'll go with you to the audition. I'd say dress casual, but not too casual for the meeting with Dylan."

"Sounds like a plan." Kris rounded the car, then paused. "Thanks."

"You're welcome." As he drove home, Zayn battled a maelstrom of feelings. On one side, he was thrilled. He and Kris had weathered a couple of big issues and were still together. The struggles seemed to make them stronger. But then there was an underlying feeling of negativity and dread. He knew that emotion all too well. Every fucking relationship he'd been in had the same dark cloud over it. He wanted the partnership with Kris to be different. Down in his gut, he believed they could make a go for the long-term. But that dark cloud still hovered and he couldn't pinpoint the issue. Would Kris leave him when he finally hit the big time? Was Kris using him? Neither seemed likely. So what was the problem?

He parked in front of his apartment building and switched off the engine. He'd never be able to shake the negative feelings if he kept hunting for them. He glanced at Kris, who grinned.

He'd lived in the past, in his own way, for far too long. Time to shove the negative aside and embrace the positive for as long as it lasted.

Chapter Ten

Kris stared at the folder. Once he, Zayn and Nugent arrived at the studio, Kris had been given a handful of script pages. He didn't recognize any of the lines. *Shit. A dry reading. Fuck, fuck, fuck.* At least the character was like the one he was supposed to play in the Fourth of July movie—a guy whose wife had cheated on him. Talk about potential type-casting.

"All you have to do is channel all that passion into this role and you've got it." Zayn curled his fingers under Kris' chin. "I believe in you."

He kissed Zayn, then waved as his boyfriend and dog headed into the audition room. His heart hammered and he wished he'd put on a little more antiperspirant. Excitement sizzled in his veins. He paced the width of the hallway and read the lines over and over.

"You must be Kris Hunter." A woman strode up to Kris and smiled. "I'm Wendy Owen. We're reading this scene together."

Kris fumbled for words. He'd seen Wendy Owen in plenty of movies. She was a bona-fide star. Finally, he shook hands with her. "Yes, I'm Hunter Kris." His eyes widened. "I mean, Kris Hunter."

"You're nervous." She chuckled and let go of his hand. "Perfectly normal."

"I don't feel normal." He massaged his temple. "I feel like a fool."

"Why? Because you fumbled your name? This is a big audition. I'm nervous and I've auditioned in front of all these people before." She flattened her palm on his back. "Sometimes you need someone who has been in your shoes to help. That's what I'm here to do. That and hopefully land the role of your wife, but that's beside the point right now."

He nodded. "Thanks."

"So. You did porn?" She pointed to the bench in an alcove beside the doors. "Sit."

"I did." He followed her directive. "Seven years."

"No cooties?" She leaned against the side wall of the alcove.

"Nope." His skin prickled and his stomach churned.

"Hey, put the color back in your cheeks. I'm making small talk. We have to be comfortable with each other before we can do this reading." She patted his thigh. "I've never worked with someone who did porn, but I've heard you all work as hard as regular actors. Probably harder because you've got to convince the audience you're enjoying fucking the person you're in bed with. Yeah?"

"For the most part, that's true. When you're first in the business, you're horny as hell and will fuck pretty much anything. You want to impress the directors and such so you can keep working. Then the shine wears off. There will always be those who can fake it really well and some that aren't faking—they really enjoy having sex that much. I got burned out."

"And yet you're with one of the hottest casting directors in Hollywood. I hope you and Zayn don't burn out. You're cute together." She patted his thigh again. "You're honest and sweet. As long as you listen to Zayn and keep that attitude, you and I are going to rock this audition."

The door opened and Dylan strode into the hallway. "Are you ready? It's time."

She glanced at Kris, then nodded. "We're ready."

Dylan stopped them before they entered the auditions room. "I handpicked the both of you. Yes, Kris, this is like the other movie we're going to do, but it's not the same. You're initially clueless, but in this one you get hip real quick. Wendy, you're feeling more guilt that you let on and that's why eventually you two work this out. This one has a better ending than the other movie."

"Gotcha," Wendy replied. "No ensemble?"

"Nope. Total drama. Marriages fall apart, but some can be mended." Dylan grinned. "Might use that for my tagline."

Wendy smiled at Kris then nodded. "We've got this," she murmured.

Kris nodded once and followed Dylan and Wendy into the room. Unlike the other times he'd auditioned, the space wasn't very big—no more than a large living room and not nearly as chilly. Four men he didn't know sat together. Zayn and Nugent were nowhere to be seen. He wiped his hands on his pants, then dropped his script onto the dining room table. According to the notes in the script, he and Wendy were to have the conversation there.

"Okay, so." Dylan strode to the middle of the room. "This is the first big, emotional scene of the movie. Wendy has already had the affair and is trying to figure out how to explain to her husband what she's done. This isn't a fluffy movie and will take some grit." He turned his attention to Kris and Wendy. "I sent this to you already, but you'll see I made some changes. Actually, the writers did, but that's beside the point. Read what's there and if you feel the need to improvise, don't go too crazy."

Kris leaned against the table and rested his weight on his hands. He stared at the script as if it were the newspaper.

"What'cha reading?" Wendy asked and slipped up beside Kris.

"The paper. There's a story here about adultery." He chuckled. "That won't be us." He moved his arm to drape it around her shoulders, but she pulled away from him. "What's wrong? I can't hug you now?" He tipped his head to the side. "Come here, babe."

Wendy hesitated. "I—have you ever thought you might grow out of a relationship? I mean, like they talk about in that article?"

"Oh, you read it?" He turned around and folded his arms, then rested his ass against the table. "I don't know that I agree with it. I mean, I can outgrow my high school baseball jersey, but a relationship? You're supposed to grow together. It's work, but you put the work in."

"That's not what I meant." She inched away from him. "Clothing and relationships aren't the same."

"I know." He frowned, then reached for her again. "I was trying to make a joke. You're all tense. Come on. Let me hug you. You used to like it when I held you tight and we'd sway together."

"I can't." She shook her head and put her hand up. "Just can't."

"Why? Don't you love me anymore?" He grinned, but when he met her glare, the grin faded. "Talk, then. Explain why you're being so... I'm not sure what."

Wendy fidgeted and twisted her fingers together. "I've—I've got a girlfriend and she and her boyfriend are...they're having problems. He doesn't know it, but she's cheating on him."

"Rough." He stared at her. "I bet he's crushed."

"He doesn't know." She kept her gaze low. "I'm not sure what to say."

"He's truly got no clue?"

"Nope. He's happy as a lark."

Kris narrowed his eyes and clicked his tongue. According to the script, he'd known his wife since they were both in middle school. They'd grown up together and nearly twenty years on, he knew her better than she thought. She wasn't talking about some friend. She meant them. His heart ached for the relationship that was about to die.

"What?" Wendy asked.

"She's not in love with him?" he asked, his tone soft. "Like a phase not in love or she wants to be apart forever? And do I know the guy?"

"Who?" She stared at him, her eyes wide.

"The boyfriend." If she wanted to keep up the charade, he would—for now. "Maybe I can talk to him."

"I doubt you'd get through to him. He's thickheaded."

"Oh." He turned away from Wendy to hide his upset. He flipped through the pages of the script. According to the lines on the page, he wasn't supposed to cry, but he was supposed to be at a realization. Tears threatened at the corners of his eyes. "Is she serious about the new guy?" He shook his head, unable to meet her gaze. "If she's got a guy already, then the relationship is dead. She moved on. Nothing more to say."

"I—I think she does." She fumbled. "Have a guy and want to move on."

He blinked back tears and sighed. "Then she owes him the decency of being honest. He might not look like he knows, but he's probably got an inkling. He might be torn up inside, trying to figure out a way to get her back."

"You do?"

"I do what?" he asked. He glanced over his shoulder at her. When he saw the pain in her eyes, the tears finally fell. Maybe it wasn't manly for him to cry, but what the hell. His relationship with his wife was falling all to pieces.

"You think he knows she's…unfaithful?"

"Probably."

Wendy paused. Her gaze didn't quite meet his as she sat on the table. "What if the friend was really me?"

He cleared his throat. "Well." He brushed the tears away with the back of his hand. "I'd have to do the right thing. I love you, babe. Always will, but if I can't be who you need, then I can't hold you down."

"You wouldn't fight for me?"

"I can fight all I want, but if you're gone, there's nothing to fight over." He rested his forehead on hers. "I might not like what you've got to say, but you've got to be honest with me."

She nodded and together, they cried.

"Cut," Dylan shouted. "Holy hell. Cut. Oh my God." He rushed over to them and touched Kris' shoulder. When Kris turned his attention to the director, there were tears in Dylan's eyes. "Yeah, you got me all slobbery too."

Kris wiped his face, then dragged a long breath into his lungs. He glanced at Zayn. His boyfriend simply stood and nodded. The smile wrapped from ear to ear.

"Did you even remember you had an audience?" Dylan asked.

"I forgot," Kris confessed.

Wendy blew out a breath. "I did too."

"Well, I'm blown away." Dylan clapped his hands and nodded again. "I'm going to talk to the others. Stay here and give me a few." He left Kris and Wendy alone, then gathered the men at the table together. As a mass, they left the room.

"I don't know about them, but holy shit." Zayn laughed. He let go of Nugent, allowing the dog to trot across the space to Kris. "I — That doesn't happen often. The magic is totally there. If I were casting this, you'd both be hired."

Kris knelt to pet Nugent. "But you're not. Unfortunately." He focused on the dog. "We were that good?"

"I felt like I was watching the movie. Okay, so you're at a folding table and reading a script, but that desire I told you was there showed up in a big way," Zayn said. "And you, Wendy...you two have chemistry."

"I'd try to steal him away, but I know better. He's playing for the wrong side and he's very much into you," she said.

Kris' gaze switched between the woman who could be his costar and his boyfriend. They couldn't really be talking about him. Yes, he was totally head-over-heels for Zayn, but she wanted him too? No way.

"I need to make a pit stop." Wendy winked at Zayn, then smiled at Kris. "Be back in a few moments." She strolled out of the room, leaving Kris and Zayn alone.

"I have no idea what just happened," Kris said. He stood, then flopped into the closest chair. "I admit, I felt like she and I were that couple."

"It showed." Zayn sat on the table where Wendy had been. "You nailed it."

The door flew open and the four men, with Dylan rushing behind them, entered the room. None of the men, save for Dylan, looked at Kris. The chunky man stomped up to Kris. "I'm Joe Sockolove. I'm producing this film for Zephyr. Want to tell me what the hell is going on?"

"I—I'm not sure," Kris stammered. "What's wrong?"

Zayn stood beside Kris. "What's got you all up in arms, Joe?"

"This guy does. Porn? Seriously? You've got to be kidding me." The veins in Joe's forehead bulged. "Want to explain yourself?"

Zayn stepped forward, but Kris put his hand up. "I will," Kris said. "I'm not going to lie or hide my past. Yes, I did porn. Six years. I showed my backside, front side and pretty much everything else. Am I completely proud of what I did? No, but I got my bills paid. Do I regret starring in those films? No. I didn't do anything wrong. Yes, I want to move beyond that chapter in my life. I can do this role. If you can have faith in me, I'll be your wild card, but you won't regret the decision."

"You're damn right I won't regret my decision. We're not hiring you. I want a wholesome actor, not some X-rated freak," Joe snapped. "Zayn, I'd have thought you and Dylan would've found someone better than this jerk for the role. I'm disheartened by all of this." Joe shook his head and turned on his heel. "Come on. We've got to keep looking."

"You're giving up on me, just like that? All because of my past," Kris shouted and jumped out of his seat.

"You never did anything you weren't proud of? I'm not currently doing porn. This is what I want to do with my life. So my past isn't spotless. I bet most of those wholesome actors also did things you wouldn't approve of. No one is perfect."

"Those no ones are going to fit the bill better than you." Joe continued out of the room with the other three men at his heels.

Kris sank back onto the chair. Well, shit. He'd won and lost the role all in the space of a few minutes. Funny, but he wasn't completely shattered. He'd been honest and owned up to his mistakes. Unfortunately the mistakes screwed him over. Zayn had been right all along—he had talent. He just wasn't going to star in Dylan's movie.

"That is total crap." Dylan threw his hands in the air. "It's a freaking low-budget, highly emotional drama. We can make the damn thing at my freaking house if we wanted to." He growled and shook his head. "I can't fund this on my own. Zephyr isn't my only choice, but it was the best one."

"They've got sole rights to the property?" Zayn asked.

"No. I put a clause in stating that I needed the correct actors for this to work. Everyone but Trident signed on the dotted line. Odd, since I'm still a newer director, but they believed me when I said I believed in this movie." Dylan rested his hands on the table and dipped his head. "I never thought they'd do this."

"You can be wrong sometimes," Kris murmured. He summoned his courage. "I'm thankful for the opportunity. Reading with Wendy and learning about the business opened my eyes. I can move out of the porn industry if I want to. I'm not defined by what I did, although it taught me to be the man I am." He stood. His resolve returned. "But that aside, you can all be wrong sometimes. I'm not the right person for this particular picture—not with those producers. I'm never going to be."

"Kris." Zayn grasped Kris' shoulder. "That's not... You're meant for this role."

Dylan nodded. "He's right."

"You need those producers?" Kris asked. "You said you shopped the picture around. Would any of the other studios bite?"

"No, because they're leery of your past." Dylan narrowed his eyes and folded his arms. "What are you trying to say?"

Now was his chance to put his idea forth. "What if you made the film yourself? No studio and distribution to the film festivals. If the movie is the high-stakes drama you claim it to be, then you should get attention at those festivals."

"But funding," Zayn cut in. "That's why we have the studios—among other things. Someone has to help foot the bill until we make it back in the theaters."

"I know," Kris said. "I haven't been completely honest with you, Zayn. I already had a plan in place before I met you. I wasn't staying in porn for the rest of my life. Two years ago, I started to put back two-thirds of what I made from every picture. I had enough to live on comfortably and the rest went into savings. I've got over a hundred grand saved up and the plan was to use it to make my own movie. I didn't care what it was, but I wanted to create something that didn't involve porn." Pride swelled in his heart. He could do this—he could create something great from a pile of negativity.

"You're saying we pool our resources to make this movie." Dylan's eyes lit up. "I don't know why it couldn't work. We'd have to use a lawyer to make everything legal and to ensure everyone got paid properly, but your hundred grand, my hundred grand..."

Wendy strolled back into the room. "I'll put in that much," she added. "I'm not under contract to Zephyr, either. I want this picture made and I can't see anyone else in the role but Kris." She linked arms with him. "That's three hundred grand. How much more do you need?"

"Double that, but this is definitely doable." Dylan turned to Zayn. "What do you think?"

Zayn shook his head. "There's a lot to consider beyond the legalities. You've got the crew. Paying for them will get pricey. The equipment. You won't have the security of the studio for that stuff. You'll have to get the cameras, film and editing software on your own. What about promotion? You're taking on a lot of responsibility. This isn't one of Paul's horror films that goes right into cult status. This is a huge gamble."

"You know what? You're right." Dylan clapped his hands. "I've got some favors to call in. Wen—will you help me?" He tugged Wendy with him out of the room, leaving Zayn and Kris alone.

Kris pressed his lips together. There were so many things he wanted to say, but if he blurted everything out, he'd push Zayn away. He exhaled and stared at his boyfriend. "Be honest with me."

"About?" Zayn didn't look him in the eye.

"You said I had drive and desire. You told me to channel it and to use it. Down in my heart, I don't feel like I'm making a mistake here. Working with Dylan and Wendy on this project feels right. I could be screwing up royally, but this is where I need you to be honest. I can believe I've got the passion and drive to be something besides a porn star, but you're the one in this business. You've seen a hundred like me and you've probably seen them all fall. If I'm making the world's biggest fuck-up, then this is where you need to put your feelings aside and be professional. Tell me the truth. What the hell just changed?"

Zayn scratched his forehead, then sat on the table. He folded his legs up underneath himself and rested his elbows on his knees. "I want to see you shine. I believe you can do whatever it is you set your mind to. You've accepted yourself and what you did in the past. That's admirable. But I'm practical. As someone who has been in this business, I'm starting to wonder about the future. I can see plenty of times where your past is going to come back and bite you. If you're willing to take that risk and make something of it, then make the movie. If you're not strong enough to handle the harsh criticism that's coming your way, based on nothing more than your former chosen profession, then don't waste your money."

The queasiness returned. Kris ran his fingers through his hair. "I'm a lot stronger than you give me credit for and I'm beginning to think there's something fishy here. Why did you get involved with me?"

"Because you're handsome." Zayn scrubbed his face with both hands. "You're charming, sexy and I liked what I saw."

"But you weren't expecting what you saw to last. I was supposed to be a one-night thing or a quick weekend fuck, right? Then we started opening up to each other. We started taking this beyond the weekend and you got in too deep." Kris nodded. He hooked his fingers in his belt loops. "Once you realized we'd gotten out of hand, you shut down on me. My abilities aren't important right now. It's your ego. When you thought you could keep me in line because I was still moldable, you were happy. Now that I might not need you, you're running scared."

"That's not true," Zayn snapped. "You don't know that."

"No? This should be the time when we're pulling hardest against each other and rooting for each other. You should want me to succeed as much as I do you. I grew up and accepted my past. You're still living under the misconception that I'm going to fuck you over now that I got what you suspect is what I want." Kris patted his thigh. "Come here, Nuge." He held on to the dog's leash. "I did get what I wanted—or I thought I did. My plan was to follow my dreams out of porn and into a real acting career. Finding you along the way was icing on the cake. I never expected you to make me your project. I expected us to be a team. I see I was wrong." He sighed. "I'm going to gather my stuff. I'll get a ride home, okay? Don't worry about us." He turned on his heel and started away from Zayn. His heart ripped in half, but at least he'd stayed true to himself.

"Kris."

He stopped, but didn't turn around. *Please let him say I'm not making the biggest horse's ass of myself by walking away.*

"I can't stand aside and let you step into the oncoming storm. I know once the movie is made and released in all those festivals, the first thing anyone is going to say is that you're from porn. With a studio, you can hide some of that past. Without it, you've got to deal with it. The film won't get the press it deserves and they'll make you into a freak."

Zayn's words stung, even if they were probably true. "So you only had faith in me if you could shelter me?"

"That's *not* what I meant."

"I think it is." Kris stared straight ahead and walked out of the room. He wanted to believe he'd done the right thing by leaving Zayn behind, but he wasn't sure. What he did know was that in spite of everything else, he didn't need Zayn. He could live without him, but he'd never be the same. He'd fallen in love with Zayn. Would his heart survive the damage? Who knew?

First, he had to keep moving forward.

"We got our funding matched." Wendy bounced up to Kris. "We got our... What happened?" She grabbed his free hand and tugged him over to one of the benches in the foyer. "You look like we took away your birthday."

"Zayn and I split." He sighed and begged the tears stinging behind his eyes, not to fall. "He can't stand behind what we want to do."

"He's been an old fart, but he'll come around." She squeezed Kris' hand. "He's smart when it comes to the movie business. His dad was one of the greats. I'm sure he's worried right now, but when he sees what will come of our hard work, he'll come around."

"I wish I could be so positive." He smiled, despite his inner turmoil. "It's my past. He can't see beyond it or his own. Eli might have done a number on me by trying to destroy my career and potentially killing my dog, but he really fucked with Zayn's head. I'm not Eli. I don't want Zayn to make my career for me. I need to do this on my own."

"You do. You'll respect what you've got more because of that very reason." Wendy nodded. A lock of her black hair slipped in front of her eyes. "For what it's worth, I've made a lot of movies and all of them with most of my clothes on. I've worked with some of the top names in Hollywood and some of the newest, greenest actors in the business. I wouldn't throw a cool hundred grand into a film I didn't believe in and I certainly wouldn't toss a perfectly good opportunity with a studio away on some hack actor. I heard you tell those producers everything. That took guts and made me respect you so much more. If Zayn can't see the wonderful, strong man he had, then it'll hurt, but maybe you're better off without him."

"You sure know how to build a guy up," Kris said with a half chuckle.

"No, I know how to fuck him over and send him packing, but you're not someone I'm dating." She tucked her hair behind her ear and patted his thigh. "You're a damn good actor that I want as my costar."

"Thanks."

"I suppose you need a ride home?" she asked. "God. Zayn knows how to screw up a good thing."

"I dumped him." Kris stood. With Nugent at his side, he walked with Wendy out of the building. "I feel like shit."

"I'd love to say it'll pass, but I can't. When you're truly in love, the cuts are the deepest." She opened the door to a shiny red convertible. "I can't imagine you're going to get over him fast, nor do I expect you to. What I do expect is for you to channel that hurt. We're going to make one hell of a movie. I have faith in what we've got planned. Do you?"

Kris pointed to the backseat of the car. "I'm not trying to ignore what you've asked me. I'm thinking about it, but do you mind if I sit in the back with the dog? As far as I know, he's never ridden in a convertible and I don't want him to jump out."

"By all means." She grinned. "You're thinking about someone other than yourself. That's pretty fantastic."

"Thanks." He moved the seat out of the way and allowed Nugent to climb into the car first. Once the dog settled, he plopped onto the other seat. So many thoughts bombarded him. Did he have faith in the movie? Back in the audition room, he knew what he wanted. Hell, an hour ago, he'd known. But in that short period of time, everything had changed. His boyfriend wasn't so confident about his abilities. The studio didn't want anything to do with his past. He'd found two like-minded souls who wanted to work with him, despite the odds stacked against the project.

"Where are we going?" Wendy asked and switched on the engine.

"I'm in the development off North Haverbrook." Kris grasped the back of the front seat. "The condo development."

"Cool. I've never been down there. I wanted to check out the condos, so this will be a great excuse." She grinned at him in the rearview mirror, then pulled out of the lot.

He allowed his mind to wander as they drove across the city to his development. The sky wasn't quite as clear and the world not as bright without Zayn beside him. They'd been a great pair. But he had to think about himself and his dog. He'd offered to put up a large amount of money in the name of a dream. The more he thought about his situation, the more he believed in what he wanted to do.

Fifteen minutes later, Wendy pulled into the development and onto his road. He touched her shoulder and pointed to his condo. The yellow caution tape fluttered on the wrought iron rails on either side of his steps. A wide orange sticker clung to the front door. Good thing he'd put in a screen door. At least the sticker wasn't screwing up his paint job.

"This is a nice neighborhood." She frowned and left the car. "Caution tape? What happened? This is from a spoof or a movie set, right?"

"I wish. Someone broke into my house and I haven't had a chance to get rid of the tape and the sticker." He unlocked the door beside the garage and flipped on the light. "You're welcome to check out the layout of the condo. They're all the same, except some are flipped. Mine is the mirror image of the one next door."

"Nice." She touched the quartz of the countertop. "I won't stay long. You've got a script to go through."

"You mentioned our funding went up. How? Who?" He unlocked Nugent's leash, then allowed the dog to run the condo.

"Turns out one of the producers wasn't on board with Joe's stance against you. He said if we could come up with five hundred grand, he'd double it and give us access to the cameras. We wouldn't be under the Zephyr umbrella, but we'd still have the good shit to work with." She smiled and leaned against the counter. "I talked to my lawyer. As long as we've all got representation and are cooperating, we'll be fine—just like you said. When it comes to promotion, we'll have to do it ourselves, but we've done that all along. So, I ask you again. Do you have faith in the project?"

He wanted Zayn to share in his life and the experience, but he knew better than to dwell on something that wasn't going to work. "I've thought about your question. This is my career and my reputation on the line as much as everyone else's. I'm the wild card, but I believe your faith in me will pay off and I'm willing to take the gamble on us because I truly believe we can make magic with this film."

"The process won't be easy or painless, but you're going to love what we're all going to do." Wendy squealed and threw her arms around his neck. "We're making a movie!"

He wished he felt the same excitement. His dream was coming true, but he wasn't with the person he loved. Then what did he want? The fame and his dream? Or a piece of ass? He sighed. Zayn wasn't a piece of ass. He was the one person Kris would never forget. Maybe there was a chance they'd work things out. Then again, there was a chance hundred-dollar bills would rain down from the sky, but neither situation was likely. Life could definitely be cruel.

Chapter Eleven

Zayn stood in the foyer of the studio and watched the convertible until the car disappeared around the corner. His heart sank. He knew what would happen whenever Kris and Wendy arrived at their destination and he wasn't worried. He trusted his...Kris. But damn it, he was jealous. He should've been the one Kris turned to when things were rough. Instead, he'd been the one to step all over Kris' dreams.

He wrestled with his decision. Why the switch? Why build the man up only to shatter him when the moment of truth came? Because he was being realistic...right? He didn't have that kind of money to give to an indie movie and neither should Kris...right? He'd been easing Kris down gently. Or was he really keeping Kris in line and the walls around his own heart nice and high? Kris wasn't Eli. He wasn't asking, begging or forcing Zayn to improve his career. Hell, he'd tried to convince Zayn to stay out of the situation. Kris had held his own in the audition and possessed real talent. Then there was the money. Kris had ponied up what seemed to be his own cash to make the project happen.

Zayn growled to himself and shoved his hands deep into his pockets. He'd been stupid and hadn't trusted Kris. He should've been building Kris up while being cautious. All his talk about Kris being great meant nothing if Zayn couldn't stand beside him through anything.

But I love him.

Did he truly?

"So, you unloaded him." Dylan strode up to Zayn. "Kicked him out before the inevitable fall, eh?"

"I did," Zayn replied. Even Dylan knew him too well. Why did everyone else see what Zayn couldn't? Because they weren't the ones living with the hurt.

"Is that what you wanted?" Dylan stepped between Zayn and the window. The muscle in his jaw tensed and the creases between his eyes had deepened. "To have him drive off with someone else—a woman, no less?"

"No." He didn't hate Wendy. Not at all. She was a nice, bubbly person and probably a good working partner for Kris, but she'd been the one he'd turned to...not Zayn.

Dylan snorted. He slapped his thighs, then glared at Zayn. "Then why do it? Proactivity?"

"Is that even a word?"

"Does it matter?" Dylan growled. "Answer the question."

Zayn debated his answer. He could give Dylan lip service, but the director would see through his tactic. Or he could be honest and accept the tongue lashing. He wasn't getting to any better conclusions on his own. Maybe talking to someone he considered a friend would help. "I'm not sure what possessed me to push Kris away, but I'll have you know I had this argument in my head already."

"Who won?"

"Huh? You lost me." Zayn stared at Dylan and tried to piece together what his friend was talking about. Maybe he was thick in the head, but he was confused.

"In your head, who won?" Dylan asked. He continued to glare at Zayn.

Now he understood what Dylan meant. "No one." Everyone seemed to be losing in this situation — except Kris. No, even he'd lost because he'd simply wanted a support system. Zayn had failed at that one task. Love could work miracles, but didn't mean shit without trust and support.

"Then there's your answer." Dylan turned his back on Zayn. "You got what you wanted."

"Dylan." He hadn't wanted everyone to lose. He wanted to be home right now with Kris, having sex and celebrating Kris' new role.

"Look." Dylan strode over to the closest bench and patted the seat. "Sit." When Zayn complied, Dylan faced him. "Being proactive is great. There is a time and a place for it because it makes business better, but sometimes you've got to move on faith. Sure, there's always going to be a situation or two out there that will screw you and everyone else over, but if you spend more time worrying about what might happen and less actually doing whatever it is you're supposed to be doing, you miss out."

Zayn didn't say anything, but he understood exactly what Dylan was saying. He'd been so cautious, he'd screwed himself out of what he wanted.

"You said so yourself — Kris is a wild card. But in this case, that's exactly what we need. Will his former career garner us attention? Sure. Will it detract? Probably at first, but once people see what he's capable of, they'll change their perception. As for you, you've had the

Hollywood brass eating out of your hand all this time. You had dear old dad to get you started and managed to move out of his shadow because you're good at your job. The brass believes what you're selling because you've been right. Kris is your chance to prove your mettle once again because he's the riskiest bet. He makes or breaks you and you've got to have enough faith in him to go along."

"I do have faith in him," Zayn murmured. "I do." He knew damn well Kris would be great. He had talent bigger than some of the biggest names in the business. But talent wouldn't completely negate Kris' past. He'd been the object of negative press and gossip mongers. Hell, he'd kept those bits to himself because he hadn't wanted to freak out Kris, but he knew just how bad bad could be.

"But you want to protect him."

"Yes, it's rough in Hollywood." He groaned. "He'll be eaten alive. I want him to succeed, not become fodder for the gossip magazines."

"Oh, yes. Because it was never rough in Pornoland? He did adult films for seven years, for God's sake. There's more bitchiness in that industry than in Hollywood. Who has the longer dick? Who can last longer? Who is prettier? Who makes the most money? Who is willing to do whatever the director wants on camera? It's a mess, but he made it through."

Fuck. Dylan had a point on so many levels. Zayn had underestimated his boyfriend and the director. Zayn ran his fingers through his hair. He *had* to say something.

"I don't want him to get hurt." Even to his own ears, his argument sounded weak.

Dylan made a sound that was a cross between a chuckle and a snort as he rolled his eyes. "But you're the one who preaches learning from your past and using that pain, hurt and anger, to make the character better. He'll be fine. The ups and downs will happen, especially in this business and especially with an independent film, but you've got to let him have those moments."

"You sound like a greeting card." Now he was repeating lines he'd heard from Kris. Man, they were so meant to be together. He wasn't mad at Dylan any longer. He wasn't even upset with Kris. He hated himself for being so foolhardy. He should've gone with his gut, not given in to his fears.

"I'm trying to be the voice of reason." Dylan narrowed his eyes. "You need someone to do that."

"You're right. I acted too fast and too harshly." He brushed past Dylan en route to the closest bench. He needed to sit before his knees gave out and he fell over from embarrassment.

"No shit." Dylan trailed after him. "You did it for a good reason, but you ended up letting a good man slip through your fingers. If he's smart, he'll kick your ass before he takes you back — *if* he takes you back."

He rested his head in his hands. "Yeah, the operative word there is 'if'." His brain ached. Too many thoughts filled his mind. He needed to earn his way back into Kris' good graces. He also needed to help them make the movie. There weren't many options, since he didn't have large sums of cash saved up. But he did have access to a studio…

"Well, good luck with that. I've got a movie to make and money I need to find to help fund it." Dylan paused, then sat beside him. "You don't happen to have another hundred grand lying around, do you?"

"No," Zayn replied, but grasped Dylan's arm. "But, I do know how you can come up with it and get the equipment you need." The more he thought about what he could contribute, the better he felt about his chances of helping the film situation.

"Oh yeah?" Dylan narrowed his eyes. "How?"

"I can't get Kris to accept my apology right now, but I do see his talent. He can make it big. I think the horror film was a good jumping-off point, but he does need to do this movie—and more like it. Where I can offer help is through…" He paused. "My father. Dad has some connections and even if he's not thrilled with me, I think he'd be willing to help out. He'd get to be the great savior and look good while doing something to benefit others. Give me a day or so." Zayn nodded, more to himself than to Dylan. "I'll come through."

"I'm sure you will." Dylan snorted. "You're really hung up on Kris, aren't you? Beyond all that crap about protecting him and not wanting to see him hurt, you're really in love with him and it's got you running scared."

He stared at his friend. Time to be completely honest. "You have *no* idea. The last person I got this close to was Eli. Look how that turned out." He winced. Even thinking about his past with Eli hurt. He'd opened so many raw spots in Zayn's soul. Being with Kris helped ease some of the ache and Zayn wanted to heal the rest of the way. He wanted to be with Kris.

"Kris isn't Eli."

Talk about the obvious. No one was like Eli. Then again, no one was like Kris.

"I know that now. I wish I hadn't been so blind." He scratched his forehead, then stood. He'd been blind and way too scared for his own good. He needed to face his fears—all of them. He'd never be the man he should be if he didn't stand up to his demons. No more hiding or running. "So you're up to what, eight hundred grand?

Isn't that enough? Close?" He turned his back to the main portion of the studio building. "Maybe?"

"It's probably more than enough, but I'll have to get Wendy to take a pay cut." Dylan bobbed his head. "I'm betting she'll agree, but it's not my idea of fun to have to ask. She deserves her going rate just as much as Kris."

The actors did deserve their pay. So did Dylan. He nodded to himself again. "Bank on another couple hundred and I'll get back to you." He grinned at Dylan. "I've got a great plan." *If I can get the rest of it to work out.*

"Do it for the boy. I'm betting he's just as in love with you as you are with him." Dylan waved. "Call me." He strolled away, his step light. He whistled a tune Zayn didn't know and disappeared around the corner.

Zayn turned his attention back to the parking lot and stared at the expanse of black asphalt for a little longer, then slid his phone from his pocket. He'd have to face the rest of his demons if he was going to win the love of his life back. He pressed the buttons to connect the call, then gulped.

After four rings, he got an answer.

"This is John Mason."

Hearing his father speak sent a shiver down Zayn's spine and not in a good way. "Dad." God. He felt like a kid again, asking for lunch money or a tiny bit of his father's time. "How've you been?"

"You only call me when you want something." That was his father — curt and to the point.

"Can we talk?" Zayn managed.

"About?"

"A lot of stuff. It's time." He hoped his father understood what he meant. If he had to do much more explaining, he'd lose his nerve.

"Oh?" The line went silent.

He wobbled on his feet. Had Dear Old Dad hung up on him? Probably. He checked the display on his phone, then pressed the device to his ear again. "Dad?"

"Well," his father said. "I've got an hour before my next meeting. I might have to be late. Come to the studio and we'll talk."

Zayn blew out a ragged breath. He could do this. He could go to his father and talk out their issues. He could. Although he wanted to move, his feet refused to cooperate. Shit. If he wanted to help Kris and potentially get their relationship going again, he needed to speak with his dad in person. He forced himself to go forward to the parking lot. When he reached his car, he climbed behind the wheel.

Having this discussion shouldn't have to be so hard. John Mason was his father. He made the short trek down the road to the MSR Studios. His father prided himself on building a small but reliable studio created solely for the purpose of making well-crafted movies and featurettes. He turned into the parking lot, then parked in the visitor's lot. When he reached the main gate, the guard asked for his identification. Although the guard didn't believe him at first, the call from the front desk eased Zayn's passage into the building. He waved at the guard, then headed inside. His heart beat a wild tattoo and he wiped his sweaty hands on his pants legs. Shit.

"This is for Kris," he mumbled. "Kris." Would his boyfriend appreciate the gesture? He'd just have to wait and see. He stopped at the front desk. "Hi, Lola. I'm here to see Mr. Mason."

"Aren't you Mr. Mason?" the receptionist asked. She rolled her eyes. "I never did get why you and your dad don't talk. He's waiting for you. Go upstairs. You know where his office is."

"Thanks." He paused. He had to test out part of his speech on someone before he saw his father. "Have you ever wanted to meet someone's expectations, but you have no idea how to do it? That's the main point between me and my father." And with Kris, to be honest. "I will never be a director, no matter how hard I try. I can't do it. I'm a casting director. To my dad, that's not the same. We try to talk and arguments come out." And Kris could be more than Zayn gave him credit for — once he believed in himself, they'd both be able to grow.

"You're a director, just not the exact same kind." She shrugged. "Maybe that's the point. You can't see eye to eye because you're too much alike."

"Ha." He shook his head. "Never mind. Thanks for the help." He smiled, waved, then headed up the main staircase to his father's office. He stopped outside the thick wooden door and shook out his hands. He closed his eyes and counted to ten to calm down. Nothing seemed to be working.

"You're never going to walk in if you don't stop dancing," his father said from the other side of the door.

"Huh? How?" Zayn stared at the closed door. "When did you put in that security camera?" He didn't see one, but he knew his father. There were cameras everywhere.

"I know you, Zayn. Get in here." The door opened and John Mason sat behind a massive wooden desk. A lamp dangled above his head, sending rainbow of color around his father. Only fifty-eight, his father was the picture of health and vitality. Hell, if someone didn't know his actual age, they might have guessed him to be at least twenty years younger. There were streaks of gray at his temples and a few lines crinkled around his eyes, but otherwise, he didn't look his age.

"So." John leaned forward on his desk and folded his arms. "You're back."

"I am." He hesitated at the door. "May I come in?" At least he remembered his manners. He'd forgotten the other dozen things he wanted to say.

"You may." John nodded. He furrowed his eyebrows. "You mentioned wanting to talk. Anything in particular on your mind?"

"Yes." Zayn crossed the room. He touched the back of one of the leather chairs in front of the desk. "May I sit?" He needed something for stability.

"Zayn, I'm your father. You're welcome to sit wherever you want in my office—save for my chair. Park it." John groaned. "Talk."

Zayn perched on the edge of the chair. His knee bobbed and the clamminess returned to his hands. He wasn't sure where to start. Instead of trying to overanalyze, he began talking. "You asked me if I'd called you because I wanted something. Yes and no. Yes, I do want something, but not what you think." Tension radiated up and down his back. "I want to know why I'm not good enough for you." Holy shit. He'd actually said the words he was afraid to speak. "I mean…"

"Who says I'm not proud of you?" John replied. His expression remained stiff. "I never said I wasn't proud."

"Since the day I came out, you've been pissed off with me. You said I let you down. You said I wasn't going to amount to anything."

"That was fourteen years ago." John smacked his hands on the desk. "I was in shock and I believe you were going run off with not only your friend Robert, but a girl named Tiffany."

He sighed. He'd forgotten every detail of that night. He'd thought he loved Tiff but Robert made him happy too. Unfortunately, his choice of partners wasn't the problem — not right now. "You never took those words back."

"I couldn't. You only come home for Christmas, birthdays and when your mother was in the hospital. We don't get to see you. I've tried to call you, but I never get my calls returned. If I'd have tried to talk to you, then you would've done like always and run."

"That's not true. I have a log in my phone of all my calls. Your number is never on it." Zayn shook his head. "I wanted you to call."

"Okay, sit." John lowered his voice. "Sit down."

Zayn complied. He wanted to scream. All the pent up rage and frustration boiled just beneath the surface.

"First, I'm very proud of you. Every one of the movies you've worked on is in my personal library. Lola makes sure we have a copy the day the movie releases on multiple platforms. Second, I was upset about you being gay, but not any longer. It took me some time to adjust what you'd told me, but I accept you because you're my son and because I love you. You're a wonderful casting director. I've never argued with any of your choices."

Zayn pressed his lips together to keep his jaw from going slack. *No freaking way.* Shock spiraled through him. His father had the movies he'd worked on, on DVD?

"I want you to be happy, Zayn. Since I'm being honest, I hope you're no longer seeing that Eli. He calls me on a regular basis, informing me he's still in love with you." John leaned back in his seat. "I've also heard you found someone who isn't Eli. In the porn industry?"

Shit. *Here it comes.* Zayn flattened his hands on his knees. "Dad, his name is Kris Hunter. He's a very nice guy. I met him after an audition. He's getting out of porn." He hadn't meant to blurt everything out quite like that, but the truth was free.

"I know."

Zayn opened his mouth to argue, then shut it as he processed his dad's words. His father knew about Kris? How?

"Do you honestly think I don't know what goes on at the other studios? I knew about Eli. If I'm still correct, he's being blackballed pretty much everywhere. He's been a shit to every studio head I know. I'd hoped he'd finally decided to move on and leave Hollywood. He can't act. Have you decided to move on from him? Permanently?"

"Yes," Zayn replied with complete confidence. "That's part of what I wanted to talk to you about."

"One thing at a time." John sighed. "No more Eli. Thank God." He pressed a button on his desk. "Lola, any more calls from Eli—you know—are to be ignored." He didn't give her a chance to answer and instead laced his fingers together. "Second thing, I don't care whose ass you stick your dick into as long as you're safe. Your mother and I have only one son and we'd like him to outlive us."

"Dad?"

"I'm serious. I see no point in arguing. You're a grown man. If you're happy, then I'm happy. Is this guy—the porn guy—the one you're interested in?"

"He is." Zayn finally relaxed a bit. He couldn't believe what he'd heard, but he refused to ignore the chance to build a new relationship with his dad.

"Since you brought up Kris, let's discuss him. I got a call from Dylan about ten minutes ago. Said he needed funding for a picture. Said he'd given you the green light to cast the thing, but Zephyr turned down your choices." John crooked one eyebrow. "Is that true?"

"Every word." No doubts. His excitement grew. "I did my job and they weren't happy."

"Who'd you cast that caused the bitch fit?"

"Kris." He gripped the arms of the chair with clammy hands. "I know it's a long shot, but he's the best for the role."

"Because he's your boyfriend?" John asked. "That's hardly a good reason for casting someone."

"Because he's the right man for the job. He's got what it takes to be the character. He outperformed the other actors competing for the role. The problem was his past in porn. The studio refused to back someone who was in that business. It promoted the wrong image." Zayn gripped the arms of the chair. "Image aside, Kris is the right build, the right temperament and the right actor for the role." He sounded like he was begging. Maybe he was. Getting the casting right would make or break the film. If he screwed up, the film could sink. He believed in his talents too much to let the movie fail.

"What, then, does Dylan need?"

"The high end? Studio backing. Low end? A couple hundred grand." Zayn adjusted his grip on the armrests. "Is there any equipment or soundstages here that you don't have a use for?" He'd never begged his father for any of that stuff, but he believed in the movie.

John didn't speak for a long while. He folded his hands in front of his mouth. He kept his gaze downcast.

The longer his father stayed quiet, the more Zayn's heart sank. They'd made a breakthrough on the relationship front, but on the business front...

"Dad, I — I'm sorry. We planned to make the film in a strictly independent form, but I haven't the first clue how to get funding. I've always had the studio for safety."

"I know." John shifted his gaze to Zayn. "Well, I've read the script. Suffice it to say, the writers outdid themselves. The characters are rich and the plot works on many levels. I wish you'd have come to me to begin with on the project and saved yourself the hassle. That said, I'm not sold on the porn kid as the lead. It's risky." He held up both hands, stopping anything Zayn might have said. "Let me finish. He's one of your famed wild cards. I know from your history that those wild cards work out. I'm willing to produce this movie. I'll have legal draw up the necessary forms, but I want this movie made. I want your name in the credits, Dylan directing it and Kris Hunter starring in it. Understood?"

Zayn nearly fell out of the chair. "You'd do that?"

"For you and for the film. I can't stand aside and let a good movie not get made." John stood and rounded the desk. "I'm proud of you, kid." He engulfed Zayn in a hug. "Bet you never thought this would happen."

"Not a chance." He hugged his father. "Really."

"We're both older and wiser." John clapped Zayn on the back. "Get with Dylan on a tentative filming schedule, round up the actors and have his legal team get in touch with mine. I want to see this film completed by the end of the year. We've got film fests to prepare for." His eyes sparkled. "Yes?"

"Yes." Zayn shook hands with his father. "I will."

"You'll also bring that boyfriend of yours around this weekend. Your mother and I would like to meet him, have dinner, show off embarrassing baby pictures..." John laughed. "You know?"

"I'll see what I can do. I'll call you. Same number as today." Zayn waved, then bounced out of his dad's office. One thing he'd wanted to fix was fixable. He ran to the parking lot and phoned Dylan with the news.

"You're shitting me." Dylan laughed and whooped. "Holy fucking shit. MSR is going to produce the film. I never thought...wow. You really worked things out with the old man."

"I did."

"What about Kris?" Dylan asked.

"Too early to tell. I'm giving him the evening to cool down. I cut him deep. If he even wants to talk to me in a text, I'd be shocked." He pinched the bridge of his nose. "I'll figure something out."

"I know you will."

Zayn rehashed the rest of the business portion of the meeting to Dylan and gave him the expected phone numbers. When he was done with the call, he pressed the phone to his chest. He needed to talk to Kris. Needed to work things out. Damn.

He swiped his thumb across the screen and brought up the texting app. "What do I say that won't sound like I'm being a dick?"

I know you're mad right now, but can we talk?

He hit send before he gave himself the chance to change his mind. Even after a few hours, he missed Kris and the dog. He wanted to snuggle up to Kris and share his good news—about the movie, but mostly about his father. The man had mellowed with age.

The phone pinged, signaling a return message. He braced himself for a *fuck you* or *get bent*. Instead, the screen read,

When?

His hands shook as he typed.

How about tonight?

He'd be lucky if Kris agreed and he prayed to whomever was listening to help his cause.

Kris answered after a long moment.

Gotta meet with PD in an hour. How about @8?

Meet with the cops? Had there been a break in the case? He wanted to ask a hundred questions, but instead, typed a simple answer.

Sure. I'll be there.

Zayn tossed his phone onto the passenger seat, then tipped his face to the sky. His prayers had been answered. Now he had to make things right between him and Kris. If the love he felt in his heart was real, then they'd weather the storm. He had faith.

* * * *

Four hours later, Zayn pulled to a stop in Kris' driveway. He'd showered, shaved, put on cologne and wore his favorite pullover. He'd also sorted out the funding situation with Dylan. The rest of the movie problems were between the two legal teams. As for his relationship issues, it was time to see Kris. He tucked the bottle of wine under his arm, then locked his car and headed to the front door. The lights flickered in the neighboring condo. The bare spot in the grass from where Nugent had destroyed the lawn was no longer visible.

Zayn pressed the button for the doorbell and prepared himself for the worst.

Kris opened the door and Nugent barreled toward him. The dog stopped before actually going through the screen, but he barked up a storm.

"Hi." Kris twisted the knob. "We haven't gone for a walk yet. Been a crazy day."

"I'm sure. May I come in?" He tried to hide the shaking in his hands. "This is for you. Red. Bottled a couple years ago. Should be smooth." He was babbling.

Kris nodded and accepted the wine. "Thanks."

Once inside the condo, Zayn brushed against Kris. The unmistakable sizzle shot through his veins. Hell. If they were about to split up for good, he'd have to get over the man who made his heart beat. Please, God, don't let them be splitting up.

"So, I mentioned the cops." Kris waved his hand over papers on the table, then placed the wine next to the pages. "Seems the meat was poisoned. Wasn't by Eli. They nabbed him today. He confessed to breaking in and leaving the book. I guess he thought if he acted like a lunatic, he'd convince you to go back to him." He glanced at Zayn, then chuckled. "The things we do for love."

"Not a chance in hell I'm going back to him." Zayn patted Nugent's head. "I'm glad the meat was removed before Nuge started eating it."

"That's the other thing. The meat was planted by my neighbor."

"Henry?" Zayn blurted. "Why?" What in the hell would Henry gain by trying to kill Nugent?

"The cops grabbed him this morning. Seems he thought if he killed my dog, he'd get back at me for taking the dog from him. Somehow he believed I had won the dog over to spite him." Kris shrugged.

"Nugent spent more time on that chain than he did in the condo. They rarely fed him and never bathed him. I felt sorry for him and kind of built up a kinship. When Henry said 'take him', I did. No malice involved. I wanted to save the dog."

"You did a great thing."

"We saved each other, so it worked out for everyone. Anyway, he's been arrested for breaking and entering as well as animal cruelty." Kris sank onto the arm of the couch. "Wendy brought me home and pretty much once she left, the cops called me and I've been dealing with that crap since." His shoulders slumped. "It's a lot to go through."

"It is." Not that him coming over would ease much of anything. He'd probably only make things worse.

"Now you're here." Kris managed a smile, albeit a weak one. "I'm sorry I can't live up to your expectations. I'm not sure what you wanted from me, but I understand why you did it."

"I don't think you do." Zayn dropped to his knees beside the dog. He stroked Nugent's fur for support and calm. If he didn't start talking now, he'd never get the words out. "First, we have to step back a bit. Follow me here. The thing with Eli was a little more complicated than it seems. Because of him, I learned not to trust. He cheated on me with damn near everyone in the state of California. Not only did I not trust him, but I lost faith in myself."

"He's a bastard."

"He messed with my head. When I gave him power, through my own fear, I let my thoughts get the better of me. I was afraid that if you got out there and promoted this movie, the critics wouldn't see your body of work. They'd see your body and the porn work. I didn't want you to get hurt, but I really was protecting myself. You're not just a wild card. You're one hell of an actor. To do what you've done in the porn industry is pretty great. Then you move into the mainstream and you're even better. You became everything Eli ever wanted to be and I freaked out because I was afraid you'd realize I'll never be more than a casting director. You'll want some high-powered actor or something and I won't be able to compete. I love you, Kris. Crazy as that might seem, but I do and I was scared I'd lose you. I can't go through what I did with Eli with you, especially not you. You have so much play here. My heart is in your hands."

Kris picked at the skin on his thumb. "You love me?" He didn't sound convinced. "And that's how you show it?"

"I do." Zayn would rip his heart out of his chest and offer up his soul to Kris if asked. "That's what scared me the most. I've been able to walk away from everyone else, but not you. I pushed you away and once you left that studio, I shattered." He grasped Kris' hands. "You have every right to hate me. I said all the things I claimed I wouldn't say and acted like a dick."

"But you love me?" Kris frowned. "I lied. I don't understand."

"In a moment of panic, I allowed the demons from my past to take over. I knew my heart and my feelings, but I ignored it. I thought if I pushed you away first, the split wouldn't hurt as much. I was wrong." How was he going to make Kris understand?

"You're the reason the movie's getting made, aren't you?" Kris tugged his hands away from Zayn. "You called MSR. Tell me it wasn't in an attempt to make me feel indebted to you."

"No." God damn it. So many other people had fucked them both in the head. "That wasn't the case. There's another long story there, but the short version is I believe in the film. Dylan directing, you and Wendy starring…it *will* be a hit. No matter where it's made — at Zephyr, MSR or even totally indie, it's a strong showing."

"It's your dad's company," Kris snapped.

"True. He asked me if I was begging for the funding because I wanted to impress you. I was honest. I want you back in my life and I want you to be happy, but what I want isn't important. You deserve the chance to show the world what you're made of — with your clothes on. This is your chance and I'm not going to let you lose it because I was a dick and a few suits got freaked out."

Kris exhaled and shook his head. He chuckled, but Zayn couldn't tell if he was happy or upset. Kris finally met Zayn's gaze. "I will never understand you — not completely — but I'm glad you're on my side. I'm glad you're honest with me, even when I can see it's killing you." He leaned forward and kissed Zayn on the lips. "Just promise me when this is all over that the love you feel right now will still be mine."

"Without a doubt."

Chapter Twelve

Kris sighed again and massaged his forehead. He'd been through so much in a short period of time. His head ached. First the crap with his neighbor, then Zayn's invasive ex-boyfriend, then Zayn himself. The movie wasn't even on Kris' radar. He needed time to process what Zayn had said. He was shocked and overwhelmed, but wanted to be excited. Instead, he held himself in check. If he'd learned anything in the film-making business, it was that plans, no matter how concrete, could be changed in an instant. Hell, having Zayn change his mind and leave hurt Kris to his core. He believed Zayn's confession, but the hurt lingered.

Still, Zayn was there.

"Will you stay tonight?" Kris asked.

"If you'll let me." Zayn gripped Kris' thigh. "I did a lot of damage today. Words can fix some of the problems, but not all."

"I want you to be here." He leaned forward and kissed Zayn on the lips. They'd kissed earlier that day, but those hours seemed so long ago.

"Good," Zayn said between kisses. "I've wanted to do this all day." He leaned up between Kris' knees and caressed the growing bulge in Kris' pajama pants. He didn't give Kris any time to change his mind before he opened the flap on the pants and eased Kris' cock out.

"Oh Jesus." Kris threaded his fingers into Zayn's hair. "You don't have to do that."

"Sure I do. I want to. This is one hot cock." Zayn flicked his tongue over the blunt head of Kris' dick, then swallowed him to the root. He buried his nose in Kris' pubic hairs.

Kris shuddered. On the porn set, he'd need at least fifteen minutes of licking before the heat started. With Zayn, the heat flowed through his veins almost instantly. He scooted down in his seat and splayed his legs. He guided Zayn up and down on his dick, setting the pace, but leaned his head back onto the couch and closed his eyes.

After such a tidal wave of emotion that day, he needed to just feel this moment. He slid his free hand along his chest to his T-shirt-covered nipples and pulled. The bit of pain added to his pleasure.

"That is *hot*," Zayn said between licks. He resumed sucking on Kris. When he did, he hummed.

Kris opened his eyes and groaned. Blow jobs were good, but Zayn seemed to know what he needed. A bit of humming here, some light licks there, and a hand cupping his balls. *Holy shit.* He was right on the edge and Zayn had just started.

He tugged on Zayn's hair. "Faster. God, it feels good."

Zayn chuckled around Kris' dick, but did as he'd been commanded. He bobbed his head, rolling his tongue along Kris' shaft.

Kris couldn't think, just feel and experience. The raw desire to fuck took over. He pumped his hips, matching Zayn thrust for thrust. Everything within Kris tightened. He gritted his teeth. He wanted to hold back and milk the situation a tad longer, but he couldn't. The orgasm flooded his system and overrode his synapses. He shuddered and curled forward.

"Fuck," he managed. He wanted to pull out of Zayn's mouth, but Zayn held him firmly.

He managed to open his eyes and slump backward on the couch. A laugh bubbled in his throat. Until he'd met Zayn, he hadn't thought love was possible. Now that he had Zayn in his life, he knew what could truly happen. He could be happy.

Zayn licked his lips and sat back on his heels. "I never get tired of that."

"What?" Kris blinked, trying to keep his eyes open. Sleep overwhelmed him.

"Tasting you." Zayn kissed the tip of Kris' cock, then covered him up in his pajama pants. "You taste good." He crawled onto the couch beside Kris. "And look hot as hell when you come."

"Sleep with me," Kris blurted. He slapped Zayn's thigh. "Tonight."

Zayn sat up long enough to whip his shirt off. His hair stuck out in odd tangles and his eyes gleamed. "Anything."

"No, I meant, like actually sleep. Hold me." He squeezed Zayn's thigh again. "I mean it."

"I knew what you were talking about." Zayn smiled, then kissed Kris. "I don't sleep with my clothes on. It's feels odd." He grinned again. "I'll do whatever you want."

"Zayn." He paused. "I don't want a yes man."

"How I feel is not about being a yes man. I'm getting a second chance with the man who makes my heart beat. If you think I'm going to screw that up right away, you're crazy. We're going to fight and argue, but what I feel is stronger than any argument. I'll go wherever you want and do what you need because my heart is connected to yours."

"Oh." Kris marveled at his boyfriend. Zayn was right. They'd have all kinds of shit to deal with, but if they were strong together, they'd weather all the crap. He fought to stand and wobbled on shaky knees. "I need to lock up."

"I'll help." Zayn walked away from him, but the telltale click was all Kris needed to know. He locked the front door and engaged the deadbolt while Zayn did the same with the back door. When Zayn appeared in the hallway, Nugent trotted just ahead of him and jumped onto the bed first.

"You know you started a trend. He thinks that's the only place he sleeps." Kris turned back the sheets, then collapsed on the mattress. "He's a great heater, though."

"Yes, he is." Zayn yanked Kris' sleep pants down his legs, then hoisted his shirt up over Kris' head, leaving him in nothing but his boxer shorts. "That's the guy I love." He shucked his own clothes, then crawled in nude beside Kris.

Kris snuggled up to his man. He'd barely closed his eyes when sleep enveloped him. The dog stretched across the foot of the bed and Zayn draped his arm across Kris' belly. As he faded into slumber, he thanked God for the people and critters in his life. He'd been truly blessed and wasn't about to let another moment go by without showing his appreciation — after he woke up.

* * * *

When Kris rolled over again, he opened his eyes. Fingers of pink and orange light stretched across the bedroom floor. He wasn't sure what time they'd gone to bed, but he knew they'd slept until early morning. He glanced at the clock. Half past seven. Not bad. He flopped onto his back and stared at the ceiling. Nugent snored from his position at the end of the bed. Zayn curled into a ball on the right side of the mattress.

"You're awake." Zayn uncoiled and wound his arm around Kris. "I didn't think you'd be up yet."

"I'm awake and up, but not ready to function for the day." He noticed the tent in the sheets. Definitely up.

"I could take care of that for you." Zayn laughed and nuzzled Kris' neck. "I love sucking cock."

He wanted his dick sucked — but first he had to ask Zayn something. "What made you change your mind? From the morning until you came over, something must've made you rethink what you said to me. What was it?"

"Well, Dylan, for one." Zayn sighed and tangled his legs with Kris'. "He has one mean kick in the ass. Verbal, but he did. I was in the midst of moping because you were gone and in his own fashion, he convinced me my problems weren't nearly as big as I'd thought. He also made me see I had other demons I had to deal with before I could make a life with you."

"Like?"

"My father."

"Oh." They'd never gotten around to discussing Zayn's apparent father-figure problems.

"The thing with Dad is simple, but it's not." Zayn snuggled closer to Kris and looked him in the eye.

"When I started out in Hollywood, I was a kid. I ran Dad's sets and caused trouble. He kept me out of most of the trouble, but...I was a kid. I could play in the White House one day, then in King Tut's palace the next. My reality was so skewed. Anyway, when I decided I wanted to work on films, I couldn't rest on Dad's laurels. I had to prove myself. I swept floors, waited tables, became a gofer for a couple of directors and finally got the chance to cast a film as an associate director. It sounds much more exciting that it was."

Zayn propped himself up on his elbow and splayed his fingers on Kris' bare chest. "He never said the words exactly, but I had the impression Dad didn't want me to ride his wave. He wanted me to do it myself, so I did. But because he is who he is, people thought he gave me the different jobs. He didn't and I'm glad. Kinda like the advice I gave you, the experiences of struggling and doing things on my own made me appreciate what I'd accomplished and want to do better. I thrived because I didn't have Dad handing me stuff. Unfortunately, I didn't go home much and when I came out—like I said—he blew his top. Turns out it wasn't because I was gay so much as I thought at the time I was bi and was going to run off with a boyfriend and a girlfriend. Turns out I was one hundred percent gay."

"Figuring out who you are can be tough." Kris trailed his index fingertip down Zayn's cheek. "You learned."

"I did." His eyes flashed. "My feelings for you aren't because of a movie or pity or anything like that. You're special to me because I see the actor who can nail any part he wants and the man who rose above what could've been a drowning point. You're sexy and smart and sweet. I can't change your past or prevent the rest of the world from not seeing the real you, but I can do my best to love you. I'm not giving up on you or this thing we've got going. If you want to adopt my family as your own, we're here. I'm yours—heart and soul, Wild Card."

"You don't have to do that. I have my own family. They're fucked up, but they're mine." He touched Zayn's lips. "You also don't have to explain. I understand."

"I want to—on both accounts." Zayn sucked Kris' finger into his mouth. "I'm head over heels for you. I let you down once and learned from that mistake. Not going to happen again—not intentionally."

Kris stared into Zayn's eyes. He could lose himself in those eyes. A thought occurred to him. They'd been talking about trust, but other than telling Zayn about his past, he hadn't shown he trusted Zayn. No wonder they'd had problems. One of the main building blocks of the relationship wasn't all that defined. He loved Zayn and did trust him. Now was high time to show Zayn the depth of his feelings.

"Are you okay?" Zayn grasped Kris' hand and spat out his finger. "You look...odd."

"I'm fine. Really."

"You look like you've made a big decision." Zayn's smile faded. "You're not kicking me out finally, are you?"

"No, not kicking you out, but I have made a pretty big decision." Excitement, fear and anxiousness flowed through him. "I want you to make love to me." There. He'd said the words he was most afraid to utter.

"I'm the bottom." Zayn chuckled. He climbed onto Kris' lap and shoved the blankets aside. "I like being the bottom."

"I know." He shored up his courage. In his head, the admission was so much easier. "How can I expect you to trust me when I can't show that I trust you? I love you too and the only way I know to prove how much I both love and trust you is to do the one thing I never do."

"If it's never, then why do it?" Zayn murmured. He kissed Kris' chest, nipping his way to Kris' throat. "You don't bottom and I don't expect you to. I'm happy with our arrangement."

"This isn't on any set and you're not someone I detest." He'd made a mess of what he meant. "You're different."

"Kris." He nibbled Kris' neck. "I know exactly how you feel."

"Please?" He'd beg if he had to. "I want you to make love to me. Go slow. It's been a long time, but I truly want this." He smoothed his hands along Zayn's shoulders. "Please?"

"I will." Zayn kissed him lightly on the lips. "I'll do whatever you want." He planted his knees on either side of Kris' hips and rubbed their cocks together. He massaged both dicks in one hand.

The sensation of the other erection sliding against his turned Kris on even more. He writhed beneath Zayn. A coil deep within him started to loosen. He wrapped his legs around Zayn's.

"We need lube and prep." Zayn nuzzled Kris' neck. "Can't make love to you without 'em."

"Nightstand." He bit back a chuckle. Zayn knew where the supplies were.

"No changing your mind?" Zayn grabbed the box and a bottle of lube from the drawer. He repositioned himself in order to settle between Kris' knees. "You can."

"Not a chance." The more they moved through the act, the better he felt. Kris reached between his legs and cupped his cock in his fingers. He liked to watch, especially when Zayn was the other person involved.

"God, I love you." Zayn scooted down the bed enough to fold Kris in half. He parted Kris' ass cheeks. He dribbled lube down Kris' crack. "Have I told you you've got a nice ass?"

"I try." Kris allowed a laugh to bubble in his throat. Zayn knew just what to say to reduce the tension.

"Well, you do." He tapped Kris' hole, then gazed into Kris' eyes. "If you need to tap out, tell me."

"I will." He blew out a long breath and bore down on Zayn's finger. The intrusion hurt at first. Hell, he wasn't used to having his ass breached, but the longer Zayn held still within him, the more the pain lessened. "Add another."

"Yeah?" Zayn continued to look into Kris' eyes. He moved his finger in and out, prepping Kris.

Just when Kris thought he wasn't going to do anything else, he added a second digit. The additional pressure sent a delicious ache through his system. He groaned and dug his hands into the mattress.

"Too much?" Zayn eased his fingers around Kris' hole, stretching him.

"Just right." He grabbed the back of Zayn's head, tugging him close. "It's scary, but I like it." He feasted on Zayn's mouth, loving the taste of his boyfriend's kiss. Zayn swallowed his groan. His resistance frayed. Between the kisses, the touches and the pressure in his ass, he'd come apart before they'd even had sex.

Zayn broke for air first. He rested his forehead against Kris'. "You're on the edge, aren't you?"

"Getting real close." He rocked on Zayn's fingers. "Need you inside me."

"I am." Zayn grinned, then kissed the tip of Kris' nose. "I know what you want. Breathe for me. You're wound so tight."

Breathe. Sure. Should be easy. He closed his eyes and opened his mouth to suck in air. He shook his head.

"There you go." Zayn eased his fingers out of Kris' ass. "Stay with me." He fixed his attention on Kris as he lined his dick up with Kris' hole. "I'm right here with you. Breathe, babe."

He braced himself for the inevitable invasion, but nothing prepared him for Zayn's tenderness. Instead of pushing and forcing, Zayn moved slowly, giving Kris time to adjust. He leaned forward and kissed Kris.

"You're doing so well." Zayn bumped noses with Kris. "Feels good?"

"Yeah. Does." He'd been reduced to one-word sentences, but he didn't care. He'd been sent into outer space. When Zayn buried himself balls deep in Kris' ass, Kris grabbed his forearms. "Shit."

"I've got you." Zayn inched forward and plunged back into Kris. He arranged Kris' legs over his shoulders, then grasped his lover's hips. "Loving this." He rocked his body, filling Kris to the brim, then pulling almost all the way out. He knew how to massage Kris from the inside to push him right to the edge again.

The ball of tension within Kris unraveled. He opened his eyes and focused on Zayn. His heart overflowed with love for his partner. Opening himself up this way and giving over trust wasn't the scary thing he'd envisioned. Being with Zayn freed him. Heat flowed from his groin throughout his body. His balls tingled and he reached between their bodies to stroke himself. He yanked on his cock in time with Zayn's thrusts.

"Come with me, Kris. Oh fuck." Zayn tipped his head back and groaned. He shook his head. "Sweet hell. Come."

He didn't need much encouragement. Kris shivered and let go of the last of his restraint. When he did, the orgasm washed over him. His limbs tingled. Cum shot over his chest and Zayn's lower belly.

Zayn dug his fingernails into Kris' hips. His cock throbbed deep in Kris' ass. Another long groan escaped his lips. He curled forward and smeared Kris' cum between them. "Jesus."

Kris closed his eyes again. Neither he nor Zayn spoke for what seemed like a long time. Being with Zayn, having his ass filled, was enough. He knew how his boyfriend felt and embraced the new dynamic in their relationship. Was he going to bottom every time for Zayn? Not quite, but he could if the moment was right.

Zayn kissed Kris on the lips, then eased out of Kris' hole. He stood, but wobbled. "Damn. You made me weak in the knees." He chuckled, then removed the spent condom. "That's the sign of good sex."

"It is." Kris wiped his chest off with his shirt. "Unfortunately, I must be getting old. I want to nap. I want to be wound around you when I do, but I'm happy and sleepy."

"You're not old." Zayn cleaned his belly off, then tossed the shirt onto the pile of soiled clothes. "You're just right." He crawled into bed beside Kris. Once he settled and tangled their legs together, he kissed Kris' neck. "You are the sexiest, most wonderful man I've ever met. I don't know how I managed to convince you to take my worthless ass back, but I'm not questioning my good fortune. You've got the passion, the drive and the talent to rock that movie and any other movie you're in. I know it. You're going to be great."

Kris chuckled and laced his fingers together with Zayn's. "All that because I let you fuck me?" He knew what Zayn meant and appreciated every word, but he couldn't allow the moment to pass without injecting some humor. "If that's the case, I might let you fuck me more often. I like the compliments."

"You're a wild card, but you're *my* wild card." Zayn tucked tight to Kris' side. "Best audition ever."

Kris smiled and closed his eyes. He'd been lucky to meet Zayn and even luckier to end up with the sexy casting director. The rough times showed him how to be tough and to channel his feelings. Bring on the movie and the critics. With Zayn at his side, he could handle anything.

About the Author

When she's not writing the stories in her head, Megan Slayer can be found luxuriating in her hot tub with her two vampire Cabana boys, Luke and Jeremy. She has the tendency to run a tad too far with her muse, so she has to hide in the head of her alter ego, but the boys don't seem to mind.

When she's not obsessing over her whip collection, she can be found picking up her kidlet from school. She enjoys writing in all genres, but writing about men in love suits her fancy best. The cabana boys are willing to serve, unless she needs them. She always need them. So be nice to Javier or he will bite — on command. She also writes under the name of Wendi Zwaduk

Megan Slayer loves to hear from readers. You can find her contact information, website and author biography at http://www.pride-publishing.com.